TAKEN BRIDE

THE SECRET BRIDE SERIES - BOOK THREE

ALTA HENSLEY

Special Thank you to my editor: Kayla Robichaux and my wonderful beta readers.

Cover Design: Jay Aheer

DEDICATION

*To the victims of the Dixie Fire in Northern California.
I wrote this book as an evacuee, and will always
remember the raging fire around me as I wrote.*

1

Desert thunderstorms possess an energy that can't fully be described. You must live it. See it. Breathe it. Be it.

Powerful, majestic, beautiful, and even eerie.

You can feel the intensity in the air right before they begin. Your senses come alive; your skin tingles as you anxiously wait for the storm to come.

You can also smell it. The sagebrush releases a scent as if to welcome the dark clouds. Almost like an aphrodisiac seducing the storm to come. The dust settles, and for a brief moment, the desert has a certain freshness to it. That is, until the rain comes. The rain replaces the fresh with an earthy musk as the droplets bounce off the hard and dry ground below.

I always loved thunderstorms in the Nevada desert. Summer nights were riddled with them, and I welcomed each one with excitement and appreciation for how the lightning daggered across the gray sky. They were loud, scary, even dangerous, but I gladly watched each one with awe. I loved how they rolled in unexpectedly at times, and other times, you saw them coming from miles away.

But the thunderstorm around me right now is threatening to strike me down. The lightning going off in my heart and soul is tearing me to shreds. The storm brewing is so intense that I may not walk away from the wreckage it's causing.

"I need you to come with me downstairs," Louisa says, hooking her finger at me to come along.

I'm paralyzed for a moment, but as if under a trance, I eventually follow.

As we reach the top of the stairs, my knees nearly buckle as I look down below. As insanity nears, I hear her say, "They're waiting for you."

She's led me into the eye of the storm, and the hurricane of emotions steals what little bit of sanity I have left.

Papa Rich.

Scarecrow.

They're here.

Oh my God, they are here.

I try to blink away the madness, but it's determined to stay.

"You knew where they were all along, didn't you?" I prompt Louisa without looking at her. My eyes are pinned on Papa Rich and Scarecrow down below in the foyer.

"No, but I have the resources to hire the best in the world to hunt them down. I had no intentions of resting until they were found."

"Why?" I barely squeak out. "Why do this to us? You knew Christopher and I were trying to stay hidden. We wanted to keep the darkness away. You knew this. So why?"

"Because I'm a mother. I understand your father in many ways. There's nothing a parent wouldn't do for their children. Nothing." Her voice—calm and collected—sends a shiver down my spine.

"Ember," Papa Rich says as he reaches his hand up to me. "It's time to leave."

This can't be real.

This can't be happening... and yet it is.

I look over my shoulder at Louisa, not sure what to do next. Alarm bells are banging against my bones, feeling as if they're splintering beneath my flesh. Internal screams are demanding I run away from everyone in the house as fast as I can.

I need to find my husband... *now*. Christopher will fix this. Christopher will make it safe again. He'll save me. He'll save us.

But my feet are planted, and no matter what I do, I can't move.

Insanity is a sticky motherfucker.

"Christopher—"

"Deserves to be set free," Louisa interrupts. "He didn't choose you. He was forced to take you as his wife, and then his morals and overall good-natured personality made him feel responsible for you. This is not love, Ember. Maybe it's devotion at most, but not love. You are just as bad as Richard. You are stealing his freedom. You are shackling him to your broken self. *You* are his captor now, and I'm doing everything within my power to save my son. Nothing more than that. He deserves to be rescued."

You are his captor now.

You are his captor now.

You are his captor now.

Maybe I always have been....

"We need to get moving, girl," Scarecrow chimes in from below. "The pilot said he'll only wait one hour."

If my eyes were lasers, they would sear Louisa's Botoxed skin from her old lady bones. "You brought them here. You didn't just find them, but you also helped them come to New York to take me back with them, didn't you?" I ask Louisa, not glancing down at Scarecrow as he spoke.

Maybe if I don't look at them at the bottom of the stairs, they will disappear like ghosts. Maybe this is a nightmare. It's not real. If I just don't look and see them....

Louisa still hasn't moved an inch. She's near, but not close enough for me to strike out and hurt her, which I'm considering doing—if only I could move.

"I have the power to help people, and I have the power to hurt people. In this case, I've chosen to help your papa Rich."

She says his name as if it burns her tongue. The sneer on her face is not pleasant, and I'm sure she'll need more Botox after this conversation, for she's surely breaking the plastic shell with her looks of disgust.

"But I want you to remember something, Amber. I can *hurt* far more easily than I can help. So, leave here, and never look back again. Leave my son alone. Forget he was ever in your life. Your father kidnapped him once. You chose not to help him then, but I'm asking you to help him now. This is the last time I'm asking. Consider it your last warning." She doesn't yell or raise her voice even slightly, but the threat in her tone is obvious.

I don't want to go to battle with this woman. I'm too tired to battle anyone.

And she's right.

I didn't save Christopher. And even now, I'm keeping him captive and chained to me until death do us part.

I know this.

Louisa is speaking the truth.

I turn my attention back on Papa Rich and study his face. He's not angry or full of rage. Dark circles are under his eyes, and he appears as if he's aged in the short time we've been apart. I hurt him. I can see just how deeply I did.

He's been out there the entire time, hiding in the smoke from the flames of Hallelujah Junction. He didn't give up on me. He never would. Never.

When our eyes lock, he calls up, "It's time, Ember."

"But I'm married, Papa. *You* married us. *You* chose Christopher for my husband. I can't just leave him. I've tried to be a good wife. I have."

My voice sounds weak. I'm weak.

I hate it.

I thought I'd grown stronger, and yet, with just his presence in the room, I'm a coward once again.

"I allowed the devil to enter me," Papa Rich says as Scarecrow nods beside him. "The decision was a poor one. I misjudged. I wanted a strong man for you, Ember. I wanted one who wouldn't cower to me or anyone and would protect you at all costs, but —" He looks down at his boots and then back at me. "—when Christopher arrived that day in Hallelujah Junction, I thought it was a sign from God. I now know it was a temptation from the devil. I'm merely man, however, but have repented for my sins for allowing the evil within the walls of my home. Fire burned down that evil." He takes a deep breath, his broad shoulders rising and falling in what appears to be defeat. "I chose the wrong husband for you. I will rectify that decision now." He extends his hand again. "You don't belong here, Ember. I'm here to save you from the grips of the devil's work."

"Go pack your bags," Louisa instructs loud enough so that Papa Rich and Scarecrow can hear. I can tell her patience is thin, and she's not going to allow anything negative to be said about her son any longer. "That man—Scarecrow—is right. The pilot I hired won't wait for long. He's risking a lot by flying you all back to Nevada." When I don't move right away, she adds with more force, "Go. Hurry up."

"I can't leave without speaking to Christopher." I swallow against the lump forming in the back of my throat and blink against the burning of tears threatening to fall. "I need to at least say goodbye. I don't want to hurt him."

"You hurt him by staying," Louisa snaps. "And if you don't leave while he's at work, he'll never let you go. You'll be trapped, and so will he. Is that what you really want? You're going to drown him, Amber. You know this. I can see that you know this."

I glance at Papa Rich and Scarecrow and consider her words, even though they shatter me from my very depths.

I don't want to leave.

But I don't want to stay.

"Go pack, Amber. Hurry. We only have a small window," she repeats with more force.

As if her words are the key to curing my paralysis, I do exactly as commanded.

She's right. I know this is not the place for me. I don't belong, and I seriously doubt I ever will, no matter how hard I try. And Christopher has his life here. His work, his friends, his social stature, and his family. He has slid so easily back into who he was before me, and frankly... deep down, I know there is no room for me in that life.

But I love him.

I love him so much.

But love is not always enough. I can't live in the fairy tales I read back in the schoolroom. This is reality—as cruel as it may be.

I enter our room and try my best to not look at the bed we shared together. I don't want to remember his touch, his kisses, his promises that all would work out in the end.

No, Christopher. It won't all work out in the end.

There's only one thing left to do.

Dear Christopher,

I'm going home.

What that means, or what that looks like, I don't know. But it's time I find out.

Papa Rich and Scarecrow came to get me. I knew they would, and to be honest... I think the reason I was so afraid they'd find me is that I knew deep

down I would want to go with them willingly. This is not a kidnapping. This is not a choice forced upon me.

I'm leaving because I want to.

You and I both know that I never fit in. Yes, I was trying... God, how I was trying. But this is not my home, just like Hallelujah Junction wasn't yours. You were held captive against your will, and in many ways, that is how I feel now. I've had a chain around my ankle, and I finally found the key.

It's Papa Rich... my family.

I know this doesn't make sense to you. I know he's a bad man in many ways, but fate brought us together when I was five, and fate has brought us together again. This is how it's meant to be. And you living your life free of any obligations is how you are meant to be.

I know you love me, and I love you. I love you so very much, but love isn't enough to blend our two lives together. I've always wanted to be a good wife. But I can't in New York, no matter how hard I try. And I want to walk away knowing you love me before the love turns to resentment and even hate.

I've seen all the articles about you and me.

"A Demented Love Story" is the one that stays with me the most. Because it's true. But in this love story, our happily ever after is not the traditional.

Do we still get a happily ever after? Yes, I believe so. It's just that our story must have two different endings—one for you, and one for me. What's happy for you is not going to be what's happy for me.

It's how our demented love story ends.

I should have freed you the minute you were taken captive. I should have removed that chain around your ankle on day one. Well... I am now. You're free, Christopher.

I'm removing the chain.

You're free.

~Ember

It's time our demented love story comes to an end.

2

_____

CHRISTOPHER

"What do you mean she's gone? Where did she go?" I ask, looking at my mother and then at Ms. Evans, who diverts her eyes from my glare. "To the park again?"

I don't like the idea of her being alone, but I also understand I can't be with her at all times either. I can't expect her to stay locked away in her room all day.

"No, son. She left for good. She packed her bags and left."

My mother's words don't make any sense. "What are you talking about? Where would she go? With what means? To whom? What the hell are you talking about?"

"Go see for yourself," my mother says as I'm already halfway up the stairs, heading to our room.

It feels as if someone is gripping my heart and squeezing tight as I storm into the room and see a letter resting on the foot of the bed. I don't need to check the closet to know Ember's gone. I can already feel she's not here.

Picking it up with shaky hands, I read the Dear John letter from hell. The words swim on the paper, and no matter how hard I struggle to focus on Ember's delicate penmanship, I'm unable to let the words sink in. What is she saying? How can this be true?

She left.

She left with Richard!

She willingly left with a madman.

I sit on the bed, because I have to or fall to the ground instead. I keep rereading the words over and over in hopes that they will make sense to me. In hopes that there is some explanation or cure for the shattered heart that's somehow beating a mile a minute in my chest.

A demented love story.

I'm removing the chain.

You're free.

It's how our demented love story ends.

"It's for the best," I hear from the doorway of the room.

"What the hell happened?" I ask, looking down at the letter. How could Ember write these words to me? I then shoot my eyes at my mother, feeling rage replace the sinking hole of despair in my heart. "You let those crazy men take her? Did they threaten you? Please tell me they held you at gunpoint, because that is the only defense for allowing Ember to leave with them." I drop the letter as if it's burning my fingertips and run my hands through my hair. "Jesus Christ. We need to call the police."

"She chose this," my mother says as she enters the room. "I wasn't going to stand in her way. I'm not going to hold her captive like they did to you. Hate me for it, son, but I believe she made the right choice."

"The right choice! Are you fucking kidding me?"

My mother nods, unfazed by my shouting. "She didn't want to be here. You may not have seen it, because you're in denial, but she didn't want this life. It's *your* life, Christopher. Not hers."

"I can't believe what I'm hearing. Richard is a killer. You allowed a serial killer to enter our house and take Ember, all because she was struggling with getting acclimated to modern society? Not to mention this is the man who kidnapped your son! He chained me up in a cellar! You let my kidnapper into this house! Is that what you're telling me? Please tell me that I have this all wrong, and this is a huge mistake. Because a mistake is the only way I'm going to forgive this. Tell me this was an awful fuck-up, and you want to beg for my forgiveness. Tell me!"

"I'm telling you that I wasn't going to stand in her way of what she wanted to do."

I reach for my phone to call the police.

"Calling the police isn't going to help. She's gone. She's been gone for a while. She didn't put up a fight. She walked out the door with bags in hand and left of her own free will."

"Fuck!" I scream as I throw the phone across the room. "Fuck!"

Anger? Intense sadness? A suffocating fury? Devastation? Relief?

No, not relief. Ember should be here. She should fucking be here!

"Fuck!"

I have no idea what I'm feeling. A mixture of grief and rage is a potent combination, and it makes me feel as if I'm losing complete control of everything.

Why the fuck would she leave with them?

"She's on the run with them now," Mother adds. "Which tells me that she was part of their sick acts all along. You know the police will see it that way. She's a criminal on the run."

"That man has brainwashed her. Nothing more," I defend. "You have no idea just how sick in the fucking head he is."

I can't allow myself to believe that Ember would ever condone or be a part of killing. She's merely a puppet and he the master.

I glance back at the letter.

"She knew deep down that they'd find her. How they did, I don't know. But I bet she was scared for me. For us. I bet she left as a way to sacrifice herself. That's the only explanation," I say, my voice coming out gruff and muffled.

My mother simply shakes her head.

I point at her. "You never liked her. You never made her feel welcomed. She sensed that. She knew!"

"You can blame me if that makes you feel better," she says calmly, which only infuriates me more. "But the person to blame is you. You should never have brought her home. And you should never have left her to figure things out on her own. That poor girl was thrown to the wolves by *you*."

"Yes!" I shout. "And you were the leader of the pack. Why couldn't you have been nice to her? Why couldn't you have acted like a mother figure she so desperately needed?"

"It wasn't my job to love her. It was yours."

Her words were like a punch to the gut. It was my job to love her, and clearly I didn't make her feel loved enough, or she would have never left me. If she truly knew how deeply I did....

"You truly are a despicable woman," I snap. "I've lived my whole life trying to be better than you. Trying not to let money change me like it clearly changed you. You have been the perfect example to me as to what *not* to be."

"I know you're angry and acting out," she says, proceeding as if she doesn't hear a word I say.

"No," I reply, shaking my head in disbelief that this woman is actually my flesh and blood. "This is no act. I've reached my max, Mother. I can't ignore who you are or the things you do any longer. I've spent my whole life making excuses for your behavior. I used to write it off as it just being part of you being a rich socialite. But I was just putting my head in the sand. You simply are a bad person. Period."

"Listen to me," she says, walking over and placing her freshly manicured hand on my shoulder. "You refused to see just how unhappy Amber was here. You also didn't want to face how broken she was. She needed help, and you were too busy with your job and trying to get your life back on track to see it. But at the same time, you can't fix her. She's lived that life for far too many years to just step into our world and survive. I knew this the minute you brought her home. You can't tame a feral, son. It's against nature."

I snapped my shoulder away from her touch, stormed over to my phone, and picked it up off the ground. "She's not a fucking stray! She's my goddamn wife, and you allowed her to leave with monsters!" I pointed to my door and then dialed the detective in charge of the case. "Get out while I deal with this. Get out before I say something I'll regret."

"Christopher—"

"Get out!" I shout. "Now."

"You'll see soon enough why I made the decision I did. Someday, you'll understand."

"Get. The. Fuck. Out."

3

Agent Martinez looks as annoyed as I feel. "So, let me get this straight," he begins. "A serial killer and his possible accomplice enters your house, and you don't call the police?"

"What do you think we're doing right now?" My mother counters his question with the cool demeanor only she can pull off.

"And you allowed Ember to walk out the door with him?"

"She chose to go with him," my mother says, darting her eyes at me. "I've always felt from the beginning that Amber wasn't completely innocent in all this. She showed me today that she isn't afraid of Richard one bit."

"Because she's brainwashed," I cut in. "She grew up believing he was her father. She loves him, no matter what he did. She can't help it. Just because she left with him, doesn't mean she's guilty of any crime."

"I think that's left to be decided," Agent Martinez says as he nods to another man standing next to him, who is taking down all the notes in a black leather pad. "Christopher, did Ember have any phone calls or contact with Richard since returning?"

"Absolutely not," I snap. "She was terrified that he was going to be able to find her. All the media and attention really scared her for that reason. She believed he was coming for her, and that is exactly what he did. He came and took her."

Agent Martinez looks at my mother. "But your mother just said she went with him willingly."

"She's wrong," I say. "It might have appeared that way on the surface. But I know Ember. She wouldn't want to go back to a life with that man.

There's some other reason why that we don't know."

"Mrs. Davenport," Agent Martinez says, acting as if my words aren't even heard, "do you have any idea where they were headed? Did they give any clue or say anything?"

My mother shakes her head and gives a slight shrug. "No. Richard simply told Ember to hurry up and that they had to get out of here quickly. Ember rushed upstairs, packed a bag, and was out the door before I could do anything. I wasn't exactly going to try to fight with a serial killer. Frankly"— she looks at me—"I was scared. But this wasn't the first time I've been scared in my own home since that woman entered our lives."

"Why did you wait to call us until after Christopher got home? Why didn't you call 911 the minute they left?" Agent Martinez asks.

Yes, Mother, why?

"For Ember," she answers with a deep sigh. "I knew how this would look for her. And regardless if she's innocent or guilty, I wanted my son to hear it from me first. I wanted him to handle this and make the decision. She's his... wife. And, well... maybe I should have called right away, but like I just said, I was scared."

My mother's lying. I know why she didn't call right away. She wanted to give them a head start. She wanted Ember gone, and here was her chance to have her desires granted. If she called right away, they could have been caught. She's hoping that Ember, Richard, and Scarecrow get as far away as possible. She doesn't ever want to see Ember found. I know this.

My own fucking mother....

Ultimate betrayal.

I can't stand to be in this living room another second. I stand up and say, "Unless you have any more questions for me, I'm leaving."

Ms. Evans finally steps from the farthest corner of the room, where she's been the entire time, standing quietly. "Is there anything I can get you for dinner?" she asks. I can tell she's distraught, and out of everyone in this house, the housekeeper treated Ember the nicest.

"No thank you. I just need to be alone."

Not waiting for Agent Martinez or my mother to speak, I charge upstairs as a million thoughts swirl in my head.

I enter my room... *our* room... and feel my knees weaken.

She's gone. My wife's gone.

Something inside me tells me she's never coming back here.

I sit on the edge of the bed and inhale deeply. I close my eyes and try to focus on her smell that still lingers in the room. Strawberries and flowers —her delicate fragrance since the first day I met her.

I have no idea what to do now. If the police haven't found Richard up until now, what'll make that change now? Is Ember truly gone forever? Would she leave me like this?

Her letter said goodbye, but... how can she simply walk away from us? We have love. We truly do love each other. This I know.

But the biggest question of all, and one that makes me ill just thinking of it, is—is Ember in danger? Will Richard hurt her?

He has to be angry for how we escaped. We burned down everything and left his body to go into flames with it. Would he punish Ember for it? Would he kill her in order to never let her truly be free? Would he chain her up someplace far worse than the cellar I was chained in? Is she suffering?

Is my poor wife suffering right now?

A knock on the door interrupts my morbid thoughts that are growing darker by the second.

"I want to be left alone," I shout, hating that they can't give me a moment to fucking grieve my wife leaving. "Give me a goddamn second please!"

"Christopher?" I hear Ms. Evans's voice call from the other side of the door. "May I have just a moment of your time? Please? It's important."

I get up and open the door. It's unlike Ms. Evans to be pushy and not give me privacy when asked. "What is it?" I ask, softening my voice as I allow her inside the room.

"There's something I need to tell you," Ms. Evans says, her hands fiddling with each other in front of her. She avoids eye contact but eventually takes a deep breath and looks me directly in the eye. I see pain, fear, and even anger. So many emotions are dancing in the eyes of a woman I've come to love like family.

"What going on?"

"I've worked for your family for a very long time," she begins. "I've seen you grow from a rambunctious little boy to a respectable man."

I study her face, looking for signs of what she is clearly struggling and even procrastinating to tell me.

"What I'm about to tell you will most likely cost me my job. But I can't in good faith stand by and allow what I know to remain a secret anymore. I've always been loyal. I would do anything for your mother... at least until now. I can't be part of it. It's wrong, and you have the right to know."

"What's wrong? What do I have the right to know?"

I know she's talking about Ember without her saying so. I also know my mother never liked her and feels her leaving is good riddance. But seeing the turmoil blanketing every feature of Ms. Evans, makes me realize there could be more.

Much more.

"It all started with the straw," she begins with shaky breath. "I caught her in the act. Your mother.

She was placing straw in places that Ember would see. She was trying to convince Ember that Scarecrow and Papa Rich had been in the house. They never were; it was your mother doing it."

"What?" Her words are like a slap to the face. "Why would she do something like that?" My mother could be a ruthless bitch at times, but never devious. Never evil. And her claws only came out for her enemies who, in many cases, deserved her wrath. There has to be some sort of miscommunication.

"I think she wanted to make Ember feel like she was losing her mind. She wanted you to think she needed mental help. Maybe you'd send her away to a mental institute. I know Louisa was researching many facilities and trying to find one that would be a good fit. Her goal all along was to get Ember out of your life."

Sighing, I say, "I know she thought Ember needed psychological help, but... placing straw around the house seems farfetched. Are you sure? Did you actually see her do it?"

Ms. Evans nods. "She did it. I saw it with my own eyes. And Ember was such a sweet girl. She didn't deserve to be treated the way she was. Your mother... she didn't make her stay here easy."

I know she didn't welcome Ember, but—

"There's more," Ms. Evans blurts as if she had to or risk never telling me the truth.

I can't process the idea of my mother tormenting Ember by trying to scare her with the straw, so I welcome hearing something else. Anything else.

"Louisa hired a private investigator to find Richard. Actually, she hired a few."

I nod, not really surprised by the news. My mother has always been the type of woman to take matters into her own hands. In her eyes, if she wanted something done correctly, she'd do it herself... or *hire* someone to do it for her.

"She found Richard. Her hired investigators tracked him down, hiding with Scarecrow."

"So, she knew where they were hiding all along and didn't say anything? She didn't let the authorities know?" I ask, stunned by the news. Why wouldn't she help in having the man arrested? It makes zero sense as to why she'd keep his whereabouts a secret.

Ms. Evans took a deep breath and looked out the window before saying, "She hired a pilot to fly them from Nevada to New York. She was the one who brought them to the house. She helped them come for Ember. She also helped them go off into hiding again."

Each word that comes from Ms. Evans's mouth feels like a bullet piercing my gut. I knew something was off with the way Ember left, but no way could I have imagined this.

Betrayal.

Sick, twisted, evil acts.

Criminal.

I shake my head in hopes that blinding rage won't take over. "My mother is guilty of many things. She has her own moral code at times, but no way could she do something so awful. You have to be wrong on this. Maybe you misunderstood something or just don't have all your facts right."

I'm lying to myself.

I know Ms. Evans is only telling me the truth, but I need a moment to lie to myself to simmer down the madness that is threatening to engulf me.

My mother couldn't have done this to me.

To me. Her only son. To a man she loves. To *me*!

She couldn't have. No way.

But she did.

She fucking did.

"I didn't help your mother, Christopher. But at the same time, I didn't stop her. I started figuring out what she was doing, and I should have told you sooner. But you have to understand just how deep my loyalty is to that woman. I would do anything for her. But this... I can't stand by and let this happen. I can't watch you and allow you to believe Ember left of her own free will."

"Did they force her?" Rage begins to fully set in no matter how many calming breaths I take. "Did my mother lie about that? Did she not walk out the door with them?"

"Ember left with them. But she was driven to do it. I can see why she did. That poor girl never had a chance under this roof. She was miserable and scared, and Louisa made sure to keep it that way."

And I didn't fucking see it. I chose to put my head in a damn hole and avoid the feelings of my wife. I should have been here. I should have watched, listened, and felt that something was off. But I was too damn focused on making life return to normal.

Normal.

Nothing would be normal again.

And what the fuck is normal anyway?

All I know is I want my goddamn wife back. They took her from me, and I want her back.

"Do you know where they took Ember?" I ask.

Ms. Evans shakes her head. "I overheard them saying they were going back to Nevada for a short time. I know your mother allowed them to use her pilot to get there. But that's it." For the first time, she approaches me and tentatively touches my arm. "I'm sorry, Christopher. I should have told you sooner. I have always tried to mind my own business when it comes to your family. I hear things but try not to react. It has served me well up until now. I even tried to be a friend to Ember, because God knows the woman needed a good friend. But I couldn't be enough. She deserves happiness. You both do. And I sincerely believe you love her as she loves you. I hope you can find her. I hope you can take her back."

I nod as a million thoughts on how exactly I am going to try to do it run through my head.

"But, Christopher," Ms. Evans adds, "if you do find her... don't bring her back here. Start a new life with her. A life that you both create. *Your* life is not for her. So, create one that belongs to the both of you."

Without saying the words, Ms. Evans makes it very clear to me... I had a part in all this too. I tried to force Ember into a world she didn't want to be in. I was selfish. I was focused on the past, rather than the future with my new wife. I did this. I fucking did this.

"Do you know where my mother is?" I ask between clenched teeth. I can't even breathe through the fury attacking my body.

"She's downstairs."

My mother... how do I forgive what she's done?

I may never be able to, but for now, I need to focus on finding Ember. My mother will at least know where the plane went, and I can start from there. I'll find Ember, and I'll make my mother help me in doing so. She'll pay for what she did to my wife. For what she did to us.

4

"I'm trying really hard not to scream and strangle you right now," I say, clenching my fist to try to contain the rage that wants to erupt from inside. If she weren't my mother....

Lucky for her, she is.

"You can be mad at me all you want," she calmly says, not showing the slightest remorse. "But I did it for Ember. The girl didn't belong here and never would. You were bringing home a broken person. I told you this, but you were being too selfish and wrapped up in your own world to see it for yourself."

Her words are like a blow to the face. Maybe because they're true. I was selfish. I did want my life back, and that meant forcing Ember to live it. Was she miserable? Was she lonely? Clearly, she had to be if she left on her own. She saw Richard and Scarecrow as a way out... a way out of the prison I put her in.

"So let her go," my mother adds. "I know you want to go find her. I know you want to save her. But you can't, Christopher. You need to allow that awful part of your past to remain just where it is now. Behind you. You deserve better, but so does that woman."

"You're right," I say, clenching my fists and then focusing on releasing the tension as I let out a deep breath. "Ember does deserve better. She deserves to be happy, but she also shouldn't be with those crazy men. I might have failed her, but I sure as fuck am not going to allow her to be with those two. She doesn't deserve them either. I need to give her the option of an out. I have to at least try."

"She wanted to go with them! Why can't you listen to me? It was her choice!" I'm not used to seeing my mother get so frazzled, but then again, she's not used to people not listening and not complying to her every whim either.

"She left because she felt there was nothing else to do. You mentally tortured her, Mother! You made her think she was losing her mind. And all but ignored her." Sickness rolls around in my belly as I run my hand through my hair, trying to control the fury and the deep guilt inside me. "I thought I was protecting her, and all I did was.... Fuck. She deserved so much better."

"You can be angry at me," Mother says, calmer this time. "But I did what I did to try to fix a mistake that should have never happened. You brought your nightmare home with you."

"No, Mother!" I shout. "I brought home my wife. I brought home a woman who doesn't have a mean bone in her body. She's genuine, true, loving, and, frankly... the kindest woman I've ever met in my life. And she loved me. She truly loved me for who I am, rather than *what* I am. Money didn't mean anything to her. The Davenport name held zero value to her. She loved me for me, and I'm standing here watching her slip between my fingers. Because of you, and because of me... I could lose it all."

"She's gone, Christopher. There's no finding her. So be mad, grieve, or do whatever you need to, but she's gone. Accept it and move on." She takes a step toward the door to leave, then pauses and adds, "I'm not going to apologize for what I did. You're my son. There's nothing a mother won't do for her son. My job is to protect you, and that is exactly what I did."

"No. What you did was awful. It was cruel. Frankly... it was downright evil."

She makes eye contact with me but shows zero emotion. It's as if my words aren't even being heard.

"And you're going to help me make it right."

"I won't," she says, stiffening her spine. "Good riddance."

"You are going to help me," I say with conviction. "Either you help me find her, or I call Agent Martinez right now and tell him that you assisted Richard in kidnapping Ember. You broke the law, Mother. You'll go to jail for this."

Her lips purse, and for the first time in this entire conversation, I see a mixture of fear and defeat flicker in her eyes. It's brief, but I can see my words have finally sunk in a little.

"I don't know where they are," she snaps. "All I know is where the pilot flew them to. I can give you that information, but that's it."

Renewed hope surges inside me. "Good. At least we can start there."

"You're making a mistake, Christopher."

"I'm fixing a mistake. I'm going to offer her options. I'm going to save her from her hell but will never bring her into another version of one again. Don't worry, Mother," I say with a sneer. "You won't see her again. I'll make damn sure of it."

"Christopher—"

"Get me the location, now!" I interrupt with enough anger in my voice that she flinches. "I don't want to discuss this any further. I have my wife to find. I have to make it right."

Not saying another word, she leaves in a huff, but I know she's going to do exactly what I demand.

I quickly begin sending texts off and emails to make arrangements to take some time off. It's no easy task canceling all my upcoming photo shoots, and that alone should tell me something. I was practically burying myself with work when I had a wife at home who truly needed me. I should have been here with her. Had I been, my mother wouldn't have had the power to play her twisted mind games on her.

Am I pissed at my mother? Yes. But I'm angrier at myself. I fucking know better. I know exactly how my mother operates, and I knew all along that she didn't care for Ember. Did I really think she would treat her with any compassion or respect?

I can stand here all I want and rage at her, but Louisa Davenport is never going to change her stripes, and I didn't want to face the truth and deal with it. I should have moved us into our own place right away, but if I'm being honest with myself, I was too busy with... me. And I didn't want all the responsibility of Ember on my shoulders.

Yeah, I had been a bastard.

No wonder she left me.

The saddest thing of all is she chose that sick killer over me... which truly shows just how much I failed her.

A knock on the door pulls me away from my self-loathing.

"Christopher?" Marissa opens the bedroom door and peeks inside.

"I don't have time for this," I snap, seeing straight through this woman too. My guess is that my mother used her to fuck with Ember as well.

"Convenient that you come up here right after I tell my mother to basically go fuck herself. Don't make me do the same to you."

She takes a step inside and lifts her hands up as if she means no harm. "Yes, Louisa asked me to come up here to try to talk some sense into you."

"Don't bother." I give her a dirty look as I reach for a bag and start throwing clothes into it. "I expected better from you, Marissa. I don't know why I did, but I did."

"I didn't come up here to do her bidding," she says as she walks fully into the room and closes the door behind herself. "But I do think you should pause and think this through. You've always been impulsive—"

"Don't stand there and act like you know me," I cut in without even bothering to look up at her. "I tried to be nice to you. I tried to be... sensitive, considering you were an innocent victim in all this too. But I'm not blind. I know you want Ember out of the picture just as much as my mother does."

"Do you blame me?"

"You act as if you and I were engaged or something. We were dating. It was far more casual than you're making it seem."

"You're just being mean now," she says as she walks around me so she's in my line of sight. "And I don't deserve that."

"No?" I ask, looking up at her with a raised eyebrow. "Really? You and my mother have been in cahoots from the beginning. Perfect example is right now. Why is it you're here? Let me guess. My mother called you and told you to rush right on over here to be by my side. To try to console me and also tell me I'm better off without that 'loon.' And let me also guess, that when my mother tells you to jump, you always reply with 'how high'."

She takes a deep breath, her shoulders rising and falling. "Yes. You're right. But—"

"I don't want to hear any more," I say as calmly as I can, but there isn't much more restraint in me, so I know I sound short and pissed.

And who the fuck cares how I sound?

I am pissed.

"Fine, I get it. You and I are over, and whatever we had is done." She glances down at her feet. "But I did want to come up here and tell you I had no part in helping bring that Richard man here. I didn't know your mother was doing that. The first I heard of it is right now when she filled me in on what happened and why she did it." She takes another deep breath. "I know you're angry with her, but do know she did all this because she loves you. She only wants the best for you."

"She doesn't know what love is, and I'm not going to have this conversation with you. So, if you don't mind, get out."

"Christopher, I just don't want to leave here with you thinking I helped Ember leave. I may have been on your mother's side, and I did want her.... Well, I didn't do this."

I still look at her skeptical, not sure I believe a word she's saying. I was too nice in handling her. My own guilt and people-pleasing personality got in the way of thinking about Ember. I shouldn't have had a drink with Marissa in LA, no matter how innocent—in my mind—it was.

And really, that is exactly why I'm here right now, wondering where the fuck my wife is.

I didn't put Ember first.

Her feelings, her healing, her coping with a new way of life should have been my number-one priority, and it simply wasn't. And now I'm facing the consequences of that.

"I mean it," she says. "I didn't like Ember. I wanted her gone. But not *really* gone. Not like this."

It really doesn't matter if I believe her or not at this point. I need to leave. I need to go hunt down my wife. And I need to walk away from this toxic life for my own well-being. I just hope to God I can find Ember and, when I do, that she won't send me away.

I focus my attention on folding a T-shirt to pack. "I wish you luck in the future."

"So, you're really going? Do you actually think you can find them? If the police can't, what makes you think you can?"

"I'm going to try," I say. "I owe Ember that, and I won't be able to live with myself if I don't. She deserves someone to fight for her, which is something I should have been doing all along."

5

EMBER

The hike to an unknown destination from where the plane left us was brutal. The brush was thick, the trails nonexistent, and the incline so steep I had to use my hands at times to climb. For the first time since wearing shoes, I was really happy I had them on during the trek.

I had no idea where Papa Rich and Scarecrow were taking me, but I wasn't going to ask. I knew we were back in Nevada or maybe California, simply because I recognized the terrain—the trees, the plants—and based on how long the flight was. It made sense that we would return to Papa Rich and

Scarecrow's stomping ground, but this time, it wasn't the desert. We were in the mountains, and based on the ridges and cliffs around, the elevation was high.

The plane ride had been quiet. Neither one of them spoke to me but kept their conversation to themselves. I could tell Papa Rich was disappointed in me by how he avoided eye contact, and Scarecrow was smug, as if he knew he'd been right all along, and now he was helping clean up the mess.

The silence was far greater a punishment than if he would have just yelled. I burned down his town, and for that, I feel guilty. I know *why* Christopher and I did it, but that doesn't take away the fact that it was our home. And now, because of me, Papa Rich is homeless.

"I have to hand it to you," Papa Rich says, winded. "You picked a location that is secure. No sane man would make this climb to find us."

Scarecrow huffs, somehow seeming to make his way up the mountain easier than both Papa Rich and me, and considering he only has one leg and crutches, the feat is definitely impressive.

As we reach the top of the mountain, Scarecrow uses his crutch to point at a dilapidated—but still standing—church on the edge of a cliff. "There it is, Ember," he says. "Your new home."

I brush off my hands and pick out the thorns that are embedded in my palms. "It's so high up here," I say more to myself than anyone else. The lower clouds surround us, filling my taxed lungs with moisture.

"They were smart back in the day. The folks built this church on this here ridge to keep a look out for Indians. You can look below and see for miles, and as you just saw from our hike, it's not easy getting here. Gave them the upper hand against invaders, just like it will do the same for us."

"People lived here?" I see an old church, an outhouse, and there do seem to be signs of houses from a long time ago, though the structures are not standing and are nothing but a pile of debris.

It reminds me of Hallelujah Junction simply in the fact that there are signs of the past, of a civilization once here, and whispers of the ghosts of settlers. But unlike Hallelujah Junction, there is not a full town remaining. If there ever was one, Mother Nature destroyed it.

"They built a mighty fine church," Scarecrow says, wiping the sweat off his brow. "And it makes a good homestead for me and my wives."

Wives? Scarecrow wasn't married when I lived in Hallelujah Junction. And he said *wives,* as in plural. I still remember how he wanted to marry me. He wanted Papa Rich to find him a wife as well. Had he actually found two?

"Come on, let's get settled in before nightfall," Papa Rich finally says, his breathing getting back to normal quickly.

We follow Scarecrow as he hobbles his way to the white chapel that reminds me of the schoolhouse I spent most of my life in with my cat in Hallelujah Junction. It feels like a lifetime ago, and yet, at the same time, it seems as if time has stood still. I'm back to where I started. I'm in an old settlers' town. I'm with Papa Rich and Scarecrow. And I am hiding from the rest of the world once again.

"It ain't much," Scarecrow says as we approach the door of the chapel, "but my wives are fixing it up mighty nice."

He opens the chipped white door, and two wide-eyed women turn to face us. They cower, and I can't tell if it's because they think we're invaders, or if that's simply how they respond to seeing Scarecrow return home.

I can't say I'd blame them for either.

I scan the room as we enter. So much of this chapel reminds me of the old schoolhouse I once loved. The musky smell, the chill in the air, and the feeling of *old*. I can almost hear the whispers of the ghosts that still lurk in the shadows, and it brings me to a place I didn't realize I actually missed.

The old pews are missing, and in their place is an old wooden table, four hardy chairs to go with it, and a rocking chair nearby. In the far corner of the room, where the altar would have been, is a camp cooktop hooked up to a small propane tank. There is also a hole that has been created in the ceiling; beneath it is a fire pit that has a cast iron pot hanging over it. A green tarp is being used to try to shield some of the wind coming in through the hole, but not too much, as the hole was clearly created for ventilation for the fire.

There are parts of the open church that are sectioned off by hanging, tattered curtains. I'm assuming they're the wives' rooms. Maybe Scarecrow has a private space? I have no idea how the sleeping arrangements work with having multiple wives, and I can't see behind the curtains to know how many beds there are—if there are any.

There is also a clothing line running from one end of the room to a post where other dresses, some undergarments, and some blue jeans for Scarecrow hang. The women have obviously tried their hardest to keep the place organized and as homey as possible, considering. It even appears as if the beginnings of a chimney of sorts is being worked on. I see a pile of stone and a bucket of mud near the hole. It's a wise move, considering winter is coming, and having a fairly large hole in the chapel will make for a chilly living space.

"This here is Wife Number One, and Wife Number Two," Scarecrow says to me.

I notice Papa Rich is taking off his jacket, putting down his bags, and paying no attention to the introductions. He obviously already knows who these women are, or he doesn't care.

"Wives, this here is Ember. She's going to become Wife Number Three."

My heart stops, and I make eye contact with Papa Rich, who looks up at me when he hears Scarecrow's statement. His eyes say it all. He agrees with me marrying him. He gave me the opportunity to marry someone else, and we know how that ended.

But I don't want to marry Scarecrow.

I'm married to Christopher!

Even though I'm not physically with Christopher, surely our wedding vows mean something. How can Papa Rich want me to go against my vows said under God? If that's not a sin, then I don't know what is. And even if he wants to deny that Christopher and I are truly married—just as Louisa did—how can he possibly think Scarecrow is a good match for me? Especially since he already has two wives!

But I also know this is not the time to argue. I'm not sure if I can ever truly speak freely to Papa Rich again, but I know now is too soon. I can't read his anger yet. All I see is disappointment and even sadness in his features, but something tells me he is on the very edge of what could turn into pure rage if pushed the right way.

I redirect my attention to the two women who Scarecrow hasn't called by name yet. Both women have stringy brown hair that is braided loosely down their backs. They are dressed in worn and faded flower dresses that go to their ankles and remind me of dresses I once wore back in Hallelujah Junction. They are also both barefoot, and suddenly my shoes feel very foreign, out of place, and extremely restricting on my feet.

"Where's supper?" Scarecrow asks.

Wife Number One looks at Wife Number Two, and this time there is no denying the fear in their eyes.

"We didn't know you were coming back today," Wife Number One says softly.

"We would have had supper ready, but we were trying to ration out the food until your return," Wife Number Two adds, wringing her hands in front of her as she refuses to look Scarecrow in the eye.

The wives look close in age and appearance. Sisters maybe? Regardless of their relation, they both respond to Scarecrow the same way. It makes me want to step in and offer assistance somehow. Maybe I can suggest that I make supper and deflect some of the tension in the room. But before I can say or do anything, Scarecrow grabs Wife Number Two by the arm and leads her to the table and chairs.

"Bend over, dress up, drawers down," he says as he begins to unfasten his belt.

I see her lips tremble, but she quickly complies with his order as only an experienced punished wife would do. I can't help but glance at Papa Rich and wonder if I'm next. Is he saving my punishment for when he's more settled? It's been a long time since I've felt the strike of leather on my bare skin, but not so long that my heart doesn't skip, and my knees weaken in anticipation.

"You know I like to come home to a cooked meal and a clean house," Scarecrow begins to lecture as he doubles over the leather in his hand.

Wife Number Two is bent over the table, and her bare bottom is on full display for all of us to see. Scarecrow clearly doesn't care about discretion or who sees his wife's nudity, nor does he care that we are about to watch him whip her.

"If you don't meet my expectations, there will be consequences," he says as he brings down the belt onto her creamy flesh.

She yelps but holds her position, clenching the table on both sides with her tiny fists. Her sisterwife stands stoically near with no emotion on her face other than a slight flicker of her eyelids with each swat that is coming down in rapid succession now.

Scarecrow has no mercy and rains the leather down upon her over and over again. Each strike is harder than the last, and I already see angry red lashes that will surely bruise. Wife Number Two holds position and, though crying out, isn't trying to reach back and protect herself.

She knows better.

It's obvious that she knows better.

I can only stand and watch on helplessly. I know these two men in this room. If I try to stop it, it will just mean more of a whipping for Wife Number Two, and one for me as well. I can't reason with insanity, and that is exactly what Scarecrow is.

This is insanity.

The deepest, darkest, cruelest, and most vile form of insanity.

When Scarecrow finally finishes the beating, he pulls away, loops his belt back into place, and hobbles his way to Wife Number One. I inhale sharply and close my eyes.

She's next.

I open my eyes right as he takes a handful of her hair, forcefully pulls her head back, and says, "Now make us some supper, and don't ever do that again, or Wife Number Two will pay for your transgressions once more."

She nods and rushes to the makeshift cook station she has and begins digging in burlap bags for what looks like rotten potatoes and nearly rotten carrots.

Wife Number Two stands up and fixes her dress as she wipes away the tears from her face. She doesn't make eye contact with anyone but instead makes her way over to Wife Number One and assists in the supper preparation.

Not knowing what else to do, I also walk over, reach for a potato and a knife, and begin cutting away the rot. Swallowing back the impending dread, I busy myself in the now.

All I have is right now.

6

EMBER

I can hear Papa Rich and Scarecrow talking outside the door as they smoke their pipe and drink from a tin cup full of cheap whiskey—which they of course didn't offer to any of the wives. They also ate most of the supper that we had prepared, though I didn't mind one bit. My stomach is still nothing but a ball of nerves, and I'm not sure I could have held down much more than the couple of bites I did have dished up on my plate.

"We need to leave at first light tomorrow," Papa Rich says. "I know we just got here, but I don't like that the pilot knows our general location. He could tell the police where we're at."

"No, he'll stay quiet. He'll be in a shitload of trouble if he admits to helping wanted fugitives fly across state lines," Scarecrow replies.

"And Louisa Davenport? What if she caves under questioning from her son? I can see that happening."

"That rich bitch is going to keep her mouth shut too. Do you think she wants it known she helped us escape? Not only escape but gave us funds that will get us through the winter," Scarecrow prompts.

"Still... I'm not comfortable with the fact. And though we may have stayed away from the authorities up until now, they are going to beef up looking for us even more now that we have Ember. Nevada isn't safe for us anywhere. They will comb every inch of these mountains and deserts, and you know it."

"It's remote here."

"Not remote enough for my liking."

There's a long pause, but then Scarecrow finally says, "So, you still thinking Wyoming?"

"Yes," Papa Rich says. "Montana is an option, but a Ranger buddy of mine once told me of a very old and desolate town in the mountains. It will be in poor condition, but nothing we can't handle."

"And you're positive we can find it? I'm just not liking the idea of having my wives travel through a huge state to hunt for a town we may or may not be able to find."

"Which is why I'd like to suggest an idea I've been stewing on," Papa Rich says as I hear him inhale deeply from the pipe he's smoking. "I say you and I leave for now. It's going to be winter soon, and from the looks of the sky, a storm is brewing. We brought back plenty of provisions for the women to live off of while we're gone. The snow the storm will bring will keep them... securely in place until we return. We go and scout the area, find our new home, then come back and get your wives to start a new settlement."

"I'm not sure how I feel about leaving the women alone up here. The winters are brutal."

"I get that," Papa Rich says. "But I know Ember knows how to survive just fine. I taught her well. I'm also sure your wives know how to make do. And I think you and I have a better chance buying that truck we saw and heading out on our own. Ember being with us could draw more attention."

"The last time you left Ember unattended, she burned down an entire town. You really think we can trust her?"

"She's learned from her mistakes, or she wouldn't have left with us. We didn't have to tie her up and drag her back here. Plus, you have your two wives to look after her. You know damn well those women wouldn't dare anger you by doing something as foolish as trying to leave. Where would they go? What would they do?"

"You have valid points," Scarecrow says slowly. There's a long moment of silence, and then he adds, "We better get moving at first light. I don't want to hike down the mountain in the snow and rain."

"I don't think Husband will appreciate you spying on his conversation," a voice from behind me says, startling me as I spin to face my accuser.

"I—"

Wife Number One motions for me to follow her, fear in her eyes as she glances at the door, expecting it to open any second. "I just don't want you to catch the wrath of Husband."

I follow her to where Wife Number Two is working on masoning the fire pit with the river rock and the bucket of clay.

"Can I help?" I ask, grateful that Wife Number One is only trying to help rather than get me into trouble by telling Scarecrow and Papa Rich that I practically had my ear to the door.

"Snow is coming soon," Wife Number Two says, not looking at me as she continues to build. "If we don't get this hole patched up with a chimney, we're going to freeze." She points to the rocks. If you hand me one at a time, I'll apply the clay. I can move faster that way."

I rush to her side, grateful to have something to do and also for a way to help prove my worth. I'm sure they are wondering who I am and why I'm here.

"I'm Ember," I begin as I hand a rock to her. "Richard is my... father."

"We know who you are," Wife Number One says from behind me. "Scarecrow told us all about you and what you did... to Hallelujah Junction."

I freeze, scared to look over my shoulder at the woman in fear of the judgement I'd see in her eyes. I wonder what they must think, having an arsonist under their roof.

"My name is Holly," Wife Number One says. "And this is Violet."

"We're sisters," Violet adds. "My father promised our hand in marriage to Scarecrow not long ago, which is how we came here."

What kind of father would do such a vile and cruel thing? One look at Scarecrow says it all—he's not husband material. He's just... disgusting.

Although... isn't that exactly what my own father is doing? Marrying me off to a sick creature?

"I'm Wife Number One," Holly says. "I'm the oldest, and my sister is Wife Number Two."

She makes the statement like it's completely ordinary and I wouldn't find this information shocking in the least.

"It looks like you're going to be Wife Number Three," Violet says. She stops applying the clay to the rock and looks up at Holly. "What do you think her purpose will be?"

"Purpose?" I ask.

Violet looks at me and smiles, but then her face grows grim just as quickly. "Holly's purpose is to provide Scarecrow with pleasure. She's the one in charge of doing her wifely duty in the... bedroom."

Violet returns to her clay and reaches for the rock that's in my hand. "My duty is to pay for my sister's as well as my indiscretions. I am the extra, the standby."

My thoughts go back to the whipping she took for not having supper ready.

She shrugs. "I think Holly has it far worse."

I then picture Holly being intimate—no doubt against her will—with Scarecrow. The bile rising in the back of my throat has me 100 percent agreeing with Violet. Holly has it far worse. I'd take a beating every day with a belt over having to have sex with Scarecrow.

"I don't know what her purpose will be," Holly says. "But we welcome you as a fellow sisterwife."

"Thank you," I say, even though I don't feel very thankful. I don't want to marry Scarecrow. I don't want to have a purpose.

"Is Richard your only family?" Violet asks.

I pause as I don't know what to say. Christopher... he was my family, but I suppose I need to accept that it all changed when I hopped on the plane and left New York.

"Yes," I answer, which makes me feel like I'm somehow betraying Christopher.

"We only had our pa too," Violet says. "Our ma died when we were real young. It was just the three of us living off the grid. Pa didn't believe in society."

"I understand." Which I do, considering Papa Rich is the exact same way.

"He met Scarecrow years ago," Violet adds. "They used to trade."

"Until our pa traded us," Holly cuts in, the venom in her voice clear. "And now you get the pleasure of being Scarecrow's wife as well. Congratulations."

Before I can get myself worked up with the thought, Scarecrow and Papa Rich enter the chapel.

"All right, women. We have come to a decision," Scarecrow announces as the loud pounding of his crutches on the wooden floor seems to amplify his voice. "I'm going to marry Ember right here and right now. We don't have any time to lose, since we're leaving at first light tomorrow to find us a new homestead." He glares at me. "Ember here has made our current situation more precarious, and therefore, we don't feel like staying here is wise.

Plus, I believe God has spoken to me and told me that our journey to Wyoming is a good one."

Holly and Violet both nod obediently. They don't question, they don't argue, and they don't show any emotion other than their complete submission.

I consider speaking up, but my mouth remains closed.

"Come on now," Scarecrow says as he walks toward a wooden cross on the wall. "This is as good a spot as any."

I steal a final glance at Papa Rich, silently begging him to put a stop to this. But instead, he follows Scarecrow to the cross, which tells me all I need to know.

My wedding day is today. Right now. No escape.

7

EMBER

"Good Lord, bless us on this day," Papa Rich begins. He's reading from a paper that Scarecrow has written for him. He's reciting the same words that Scarecrow gave when marrying Christopher and me. "Brother Scarecrow and Sister Ember stand before the Almighty to be crowned under the union of matrimony."

He looks at Scarecrow, who is leaning against his crutch, balancing on his one leg as dirty straw falls from his other pant leg.

"I give away this woman—my daughter—to Brother Scarecrow on this day with the blessing of

God," Papa Rich says. "I also ask forgiveness from God in my misdeeds and promising her hand to another. I was tempted by the devil and hope to make amends by correcting the wrong now."

Papa Rich raises his arms up toward the ceiling of the chapel, which has now converted into my new home, and I see the sweat stains under his pits, reminding me of the man I'm about to marry. I don't need to look at Scarecrow to know he's in front of me. I can hear his heavy breathing. I can smell his horrific odor of body sweat and onion.

I glance to my left and see Holly and Violet are watching on with deep sadness in their eyes. I wonder what they're thinking. Are they sad for me? Are they sad for themsleves? Why are they so sad... other than the fact that we are all going to be wives of the most disgusting and putrid man possible? Will these women become my friends or enemies? Will they like or hate me? Maybe they don't want to share their husband with me, even though I don't want to be wed to begin with. Maybe they will try to push me out the door just as Louisa had in New York.

Maybe I will never be welcomed by anyone.

Maybe the fate of the ghost of Hallelujah Junction is to be alone forever.

And yet... alone would be better than what is happening now.

I'm marrying Scarecrow.

I have no choice. Not now. Not ever.

This is my life.

Papa Rich looks down at the paper again and reads, "Now you will feel no rain, for each of you will be shelter for the other. Now you will feel no cold, for each of you will be warmth to the other. Now there will be no loneliness, for each of you will be companion to the other. Now you are two persons, but there is only one life before you. May beauty surround you both in the journey ahead and through all the years. May happiness be your companion and your days together be good and long upon the earth. May you both walk under God as dutiful servants. We honor fire and ask that our union be warm and glowing with love in our hearts. We honor wind and ask that we sail through life safe and calm as in our Father's arms. We honor water to clean and soothe our relationship—that it may never thirst for love. With all the forces of the universe you created, we pray for harmony as we grow forever young together. Amen."

It's word for word from my wedding day with Christopher.

Christopher... my husband.

My old husband.

No longer. Never again. *Goodbye, Christopher.*

Scarecrow and Papa Rich both say, "Amen," but I barely squeak out the word, as my throat feels like it's closing.

My heart is shattering, because I truly believed Christopher and I would be wed for life. We gave our vows. We spoke the words.

But then, I remind myself that he was forced to marry me. He was forced to love me. He was forced to care for me after our rescue. He was forced in every aspect. He didn't marry me of his own free will, and even though he said he'd watch over me after we were rescued... did he really have a choice? No. I forced that too.

Force.

This is my punishment for my part in his captivity. This is God's way of righting our sins.

I have to marry Scarecrow.

Papa Rich opens his hands before us, and resting in his palm are two gold bands. I take the larger one, and Scarecrow takes the smaller. It's the same ring I wore with Christopher that Papa Rich had taken from me on the plane. They are recycling the ring. The same ring but a different man.

"Brother Scarecrow." Papa Rich slices through my thoughts. "Do you take Sister Ember to be your bride, to honor, to cherish, and to walk under God's eyes together as one?"

"I do," he says with a smile on his face that shows nearly every decayed tooth in his mouth.

"Sister Ember," Papa Rich continues as I consider running outside and jumping off the ledge of the cliff and putting myself out of the misery I feel and know more will come. "Do you take Brother Scarecrow to be your husband, to honor, obey, and walk under God's eyes together as one?"

"I do," I somehow manage to say. I'm still not sure if it's because the possibility of death by falling to my demise is still on the table.

The gold band slides onto my finger, and I allow the tears that had been threatening to shed cascade down my cheeks.

At least I have the ring. It will remind me of Christopher. It will keep him close to me in a small way.

I swipe at a tear. But is that what I want? Do I want a constant reminder of what I had but what never truly belonged to me to begin with?

"I now pronounce you husband and wife. You may kiss your bride."

Run to the cliff now.

Run and jump.

Run and jump!

Death is better than—

Scarecrow leans forward and presses his chapped and scabby lips to mine. The kiss is brief, but not brief enough. I nearly vomit, but before I do, he mercifully pulls away, beats his cane on the floor, and lets out a hoot.

"Hot damn, I got me Wife Number Three!"

"It's getting late," Papa Rich says, acting as if he didn't just marry his daughter off for the second time.

No big deal, right?

Just take a bride from one husband and have her marry a second.

"True," Scarecrow says, studying me. "Out of respect for Richard being under the roof, we'll wait to consummate the marriage when I return."

His words are as if the angels from above flew down and granted me their grace.

Consummate the marriage...

The very thought....

Thank God for his decision.

I've survived some extremely harsh situations, but I don't believe I can survive having Scarecrow inside me. I can't have sex with the man. I'd die first.

"Holly will be sleeping with me tonight," Scarecrow adds. He points to a corner of the room with a tattered curtain hanging. "Ember, that will be your room. Violet will assist you in finding bedding. We don't have much, but I'm sure she can muster something up." He then looks at Papa Rich. "I'm sure you can make do with your pack?"

Papa Rich nods. "Let's get some sleep. We got a long journey ahead of us tomorrow."

Violet takes me by the hand. "I have an extra blanket from my bed for you, and I know we have some straw." She then leans into me and whispers in my ear, "When they leave, we can take from Holly and Scarecrow's bed, as they have extra blankets and pillows for him. I know Holly will share."

I somehow get my feet to move, which oddly feels as if I'm floating. I'm not sure if I'm shocked by what just occurred, if I'm grieving over my new life, or if I'm ... suicidal. The thought of the cliff outside still lingers in my mind.

The strong stench of onion will forever burn my nostrils, and the vows I made to Scarecrow will forever taint my tongue.

When Violet and I are behind my privacy curtain, she begins making my bed. "I know you don't want to be here," she says. "I don't blame you." She looks up at me and smiles. "But I'm happy you're here. It will be nice to have some extra company around. It's awfully lonely up here on the mountain."

I try to smile politely back, but my face is frozen in misery. I wonder if I will ever smile again.

8

It's so cold. Bone-shattering cold.

We don't have enough firewood to get us through the night unless we use it sparingly, which sadly isn't enough to keep the chapel warm. The three of us knew Papa Rich and Scarecrow didn't leave us with enough food to survive the entire time they'll be gone, so we spent the next two days foraging for food before the snowfall made it impossible to do so. Which then meant we didn't gather and chop firewood like we should, since something had to give.

Luckily for us, Violet seemed to have good luck when she went into the forest alone. She'd come back with a basketful of mushrooms or berries. She went out this morning, insisting to go alone, and came home with two rabbits and told us she came across them in traps that must have been set by Scarecrow. Violet's eyes sparkled with pride, but she never smiled.

None of us smiled.

Sadness is her permanent, as it is ours.

But no matter how sad Violet appears, a sweetness masters all else. Such a gentle soul. So kind, generous in everything she does, and I truly have fallen in love with her. Even in this short time, it's impossible not to. I never had a sister, and now... I have two.

Holly—though kind—is very different in how she interacts with me. Strong, steadfast, and determined are her characteristics, but they all give me comfort. I know I can count on Holly and her leadership. She knows this mountain. She understands how it ticks, how it breathes. The mountaintop has a heartbeat, and her palm is the one over it.

She collects pine needles and rosehip for teas. She pulls moss and pine branches and carries them back to the chapel to fill in all the gaps in the wood that allows in the cool air. She has also placed containers outside to start collecting water when the storm comes. She's preparing for the storm, and it's obvious this isn't her first time.

Because it's so cold tonight, we all choose to make our beds around the fire rather than our respective corners with our privacy curtains pulled. I've reached a point of comfort with the women, and I figure we'll spend the majority of the approaching winter together with the fire giving us warmth rather than concealing ourselves in coldness.

The fire crackles, and I hear the heavy breathing of Holly asleep beneath a thick quilt. Easy sleep—her reward for the hard work she does in a day. Sleep of my own begins to take over when I feel Violet's body cuddle up behind me. Considering the chill in the room, I don't mind the touch and the need for body heat.

"Is this okay?" she whispers, wrapping her arm securely around me.

I nod, not sure if it's appropriate or not. But I'm cold, I'm on the ground in the middle of nowhere, and at this moment in time, I don't care what is right or wrong. Her touch gives me comfort, and clearly mine gives her the same.

"I love you, Ember. Sweet dreams," she says as she snuggles her face into my hair.

"Sweet dreams, Violet."

We both deserve them.

Christopher

The pilot is lucky I don't turn his ass in. Although he seems the type to keep his head down and just see what he wants to see—as long as there's a paycheck in the end. I don't like the man one bit, but when he got the call from my mother with the orders to fly me to the exact same spot he dropped Richard off at, he obliged. Did he offer me any other information when I grilled him? No. But at least I was in the general area. The man had to be scared shitless now that his idea of fast cash was blowing up in his face.

We land on an old tarmac in a meadow surrounded by pine and redwood trees for as far as I can see. My guess is the runway was once used—

or maybe still used—for wild land firefighters and hotshots. I had once done a shoot on the heroes who fought the mountain blazes, and we went to remote places such as this.

"If you're really crazy enough to hike out there in the mountains with no destination in mind, you better find shelter or someplace soon," the pilot says as I get out of the plane. "A storm's coming, and I'm not hanging around."

"I got this," I say, grabbing my backpack, which is fully loaded with every survival necessity I usually travel with on destination shoots.

Biting my tongue so I don't say what I really want to say, I walk away without speaking another word. I don't need his concern, and I don't need to waste my breath telling the man what a piece of shit he is either.

I just need my wife.

He's right, however. A storm is coming. Luckily, I dressed in thick boots, waterproof clothing, and a down jacket that could withstand the arctic. My experience as a photographer in some rugged and freezing locations has truly trained me for this. Ironic to think that my career brought me into

Ember's life, then chased her away, and now it's going to help me bring her back into it.

During the flight, I studied the maps and terrain and really tried to put myself into Richard and Scarecrow's minds. Where would they go? They'd have to walk away from the plane just as I am, so they couldn't go too far. No way to have a vehicle to aid in getting away. They also have Ember, and though she's physically in shape, there is only so far she can hike in these conditions. And though they may have tents, something deep inside me screams that they'd try to repeat history. They'd want an old mining town or at the very least a hunter's lodge. They'd want to rebuild another version of Hallelujah Junction. They'd also know the authorities are hunting them down, so they'd need to hide. Which means wherever they are would be remote but in a place they'd see people coming with a way to escape if they were found.

A ridge. A cliff maybe. Some place vehicles couldn't drive to give the authorities the upper hand. Richard would pick a place that any sane man wouldn't want to reach.

But I'm not a sane man. Not anymore.

I'm about as mad as The Hatter due to Richard. And for that... he'll now have to face my insanity head-on. He created this beast inside me. I'm his own creation and will be his undoing.

Now, to hunt down my prey....

"Mr. Davenport," the pilot calls out as I begin my search.

I turn to face him but don't say a thing. Speaking to the man who helped madmen capture Ember is not on the top of my list of favorite things to do.

"You have a satellite phone, right?"

I nod and pat my backpack to show I do.

"I'm removing myself from this situation. I'm going to act like I didn't meet any of you." He clears his throat. "But I'm going to tell a colleague of mine about you and that you're out here. I'm going to tell him to fly you and that woman of yours out of here when you're ready."

"I'd appreciate that."

The pilot looks up at the sky. "But he can't fly during the storms or even the risk of one coming. So, you have windows where he can come and when he can't. Be prepared to wait out the storms if need be. And that phone of yours won't work well or at all in parts of this mountain. Especially during a storm. Just be aware." He hops out of the plane, marches to where I am, and hands me a card with the other pilot's information.

I nod again, turning on my heels to leave, grateful I at least have a way out when the time comes.

"One more thing," the pilot calls out.

I turn to face him, still annoyed but appreciative that the man's conscience is getting the best of him. "They spoke of a chapel. They also spoke of hiking *up*. I don't know where exactly, but they kept mentioning 'up' and 'chapel.'"

I reach for my maps and begin looking at all the terrain and my notes again. Chapel? There's no town anywhere near the area. We are literally in the middle of nowhere. Nothing but mountaintops, ridges, canyons, cliffs, and pine trees for as far as the eye can see.

"I also don't think they were going too far from where we landed. They were lugging a lot of supplies and bags. They were stocked up but nothing but their backs to carry it all with. No way would they have trekked far with all that weight," he adds. "And one of the men only had one leg, so I can't see how that would lend to intense hiking."

Folding the map and deciding to head toward the highest ridge, I say, "I appreciate the added info."

I pick up my pack and look toward the sky. A storm is coming, and I don't have a lot of time to find some sort of shelter. I have a sleeping bag that will keep me warm in subzero temperatures, but I don't exactly want to test how efficient it is.

I've gone on many photo expeditions in my time. I've hiked the most grueling trails, put myself in extreme temperatures, and placed myself in the middle of dangerous situations. All for the perfect photos. And to be honest... I loved it.

But this is different. Hiking this mountain, with no camera in hand, in search of my wife who was taken from me, is anything but fun. I know I'm a skilled survivalist, if need be, but I really don't want the need to be. Not to mention the last time I went out in the wild by myself, I got hit over the head by a madman, held captive in a cellar in a ghost town, and forced to marry a woman who was also kidnapped and held captive. You'd think I'd learn.

Miles and miles, I walk with no destination. I just go "up" and search for any sign of life. Tiny snowflakes begin to fall. They aren't sticking yet, but I know it's only a matter of time until they do. But I won't give up until I find something... anything... Ember. I *will* find Ember.

9

EMBER

I can feel eyes on me.

I'm not alone.

"Hello?" I call out. "Is someone out there?"

I'm on the top of a mountain with only the sisters inside as company, but I'm not alone.

I feel it in my bones.

Someone's watching me as I collect firewood. Someone's out there.

"Papa Rich?" I call out, wondering if he and Scarecrow never left.

Maybe this is a test. They tell us they are leaving to see what I'll do. Will I escape? Will I take the sisters with me? Will I try to burn down the chapel like I burned down Hallelujah Junction?

Are they waiting in the woods, watching my every move?

They did leave easily enough. They didn't even warn me or make threats. They simply left... or did they?

"What are you doing out here?" Holly asks. "It's getting dark."

"I think someone's out there. Watching."

She looks toward the woods. "What makes you think that?"

"I thought I heard something. And it's just a feeling I get."

She studies the dense trees for several moments, then reaches for the pile of wood in my arms and takes some. "We really need to get inside. It could be a mountain lion or a bear stalking us."

As we head back to the chapel, I look over my shoulder and swear I see movement in the distance. "Do you think Papa Rich and Scarecrow really left?"

She pauses her steps for a moment but then continues on. "Why would you ask that?"

"I don't know," I say. "I just get the feeling it was a person out there."

"They left," she states simply.

"I know it might sound crazy, but I really feel like there was a person out there."

"Did you see a person?"

"No."

"Well then...." She opens the door to the chapel and ends the discussion as we enter inside.

I spend the rest of the day uneasy. The incident in the woods didn't sit well with me, and Holly and Violet's reaction to my feeling as if someone is out there doesn't sit right either. It's almost as if they know someone is out there. That they are in on a secret that I don't know.

Did Papa Rich and Scarecrow tell them they were going to test me?

Are they in on the plan to catch me trying to escape?

I've never been good at reading people. I never had practice. And by my most recent experience with

Louisa Davenport, with Christopher's good friend attacking, his ex-girlfriend, and the media circus... I don't exactly trust anyone.

Although something inside me tells me I can trust the sisters, which makes their actions odd to me. What do they know that I don't?

"So, what did Scarecrow tell you about me?" I ask, wondering if my voice sounds as suspicious as I feel.

Violet looks up from her masonry that she's nearly completed. Her head tilts slightly as if she's reading me, but no doubt she's just as out of practice as I am due to her living situation. "He told us that you burned down your home with a man who was your husband. That you fled to live in the evil world. He said you were tempted by the devil and couldn't resist."

"Did they say anything to you when they left?" I question.

Violet shakes her head and returns her attention to her chimney. "Scarecrow doesn't say much to me."

I look at Holly, who shrugs. "His usual," she says. "He warns that I better keep the homestead up, that I better watch over all, and that I better pray to

God he returns to find things in order." She walks over to the table and pulls some mushrooms we had collected earlier out of a bag to add to the stew we're making. "He didn't ask me to spy on you, or to test you, or to make sure you don't burn down the chapel. I know that's what you're getting at." She does look up from cutting then. "And even if he did, we wouldn't. We like you, Ember. You're on the same team as us. Trust in that."

"It's hard to trust anyone anymore," I admit.

"Scarecrow did say your husband was a bad man," Violet says.

"No," I nearly spit out. "Christopher is his name, and he's far from a bad man. He's a genuine, kind, and gentle man. He's a protector, caring, and loving. He's not bad."

"Then why did he try to kill your father?" Violet asks. Her tone isn't accusing but simply curious.

"We didn't try to kill him when we started the fire. We just wanted a way out. Christopher was being held captive. We were chained together and knew we couldn't get far without authorities coming to us. Papa Rich was away... or at least we thought he was." I take a deep breath and say the truth, even though it hurts to. "Papa Rich is the bad man. He's always been the bad man." I look at Holly and then back to Violet. "But so is Scarecrow. You both know this."

"Scarecrow is no worse than our father," Holly says, which makes me sad for both girls.

They've never known happiness and comfort. At least I got that for a short time with Christopher. Even though my life was chaos in New York, and there were so many times I was unhappy... I did have happy moments. I did have times of love and affection. I had hope. I had so much hope.

Holly and Violet, however... they've only had darkness.

"Why did you leave him?" Violet asks. "Christopher. If he's such a good man, why come back to... this?"

"For him," I admit. "It wasn't fair for me to stay. He didn't ask for me. He didn't deserve to have his nightmare continue. I did what was best, regardless of how hard it was."

"I'm sorry," Violet says as she stands to approach me. I think she's coming to hug me but stops midway as if she's gone too far as it is. "But I'm glad you're here. We can make a home. We can have a family. I promise."

I hear Holly sigh, and I turn to face her as she says, "Let's just focus on surviving the storm. One day at a time, remember? That's how we live. One day at a time."

10

The pounding of the door causes all of us to jump. We stare at each other wide-eyed, uncertain what to do.

Feeling as if I should be the one to defend us, if need be, I pick up a fire stoker and place my finger on my lips to tell the girls to remain quiet.

Another knock and a rattle of the door that we fortunately have locked has us all jumping again.

I hesitate at first but then pad over to the door, unsure of who could possibly be on the other side. I hold the poker high enough that I can bring it down on someone's head if I need to. Or maybe I should have it in a position so I can stab them...

Or maybe we should just hide and hope no one enters.

Another knock. This one louder.

Is it the person I could have sworn was watching us? Was he just biding his time to catch us when we're least expecting it? But why knock on the door? Why not just force his way in?

And then I hear a muffled voice on the other side. "Open up! Ember! Are you in there? Ember!"

Another knock and then the rattle of the handle.

"Christopher?" I open the door, cautiously, unsure.

Snow swirls around him, the tip of his nose red from the cold, and he's bundled up so much that if I didn't have a close relationship with the man, I may not have been able to recognize him.

"What are you doing here? How? How did you find me?"

Am I imagining him standing before me? Is this all in my head—wishful thinking?

The biting cold hitting my exposed skin is the only thing that is keeping sanity present. It acts like the slap to the face I need in order to remain in the present. I reach out to be sure I'm still awake or alive and touch his arm.

He's here. He's really here.

He remains frozen in place as if the storm is holding him hostage.

"Ember," he says as he pulls a scarf away from his mouth.

Christopher's eyes are wide, flecks of snow on his lashes. He seems as stunned to see me as I am him.

"I was scared I'd never find you," he says, still not moving toward me. It's as if part of us both want to throw ourselves into each other's arms, but something more powerful is holding us back.

"Ember?" I hear Holly call from inside. "Who's at the door?"

Her words seem to free me from my stunned daze, and I reach for Christopher's arm and pull him inside from the swirling snow outside. The church isn't exactly warm, but it's shelter from the storm.

I pause and look over my shoulder at two wide-eyed women who stand terrified by the fire.

"This is Christopher," I say. "He's my husband. Or...
he *was* my husband." I lick my lips, trying to soothe
the dryness that is causing my voice to crack.

I look at Christopher, whose head snaps in my
direction as if I just punched him. "I *am* your
husband, Ember. I'm your husband, and I've come
to bring you home."

I lift my hand up to silently tell Holly and Violet
that everything is all right and then return my stare
to Christopher, who is scanning the room with a
clenched jaw and darkened eyes.

"Where are they?" he asks.

I take a step toward him, still wanting to
desperately throw myself into his arms and beg
him to never let me go. But I can also see by his
clamped fists and his stiffened spine that he's in the
mood for a confrontation.

He's ready for a fight. A fight he'll win.

"Gone," I say, hoping my answer is all that is
needed to soothe his fury.

"What do you mean gone?" He then points at Holly
and Violet. "Who are they?"

Holly takes a protective step toward Violet and wraps her arm around her sister's frail shoulders. "Ember? What's going on?" she asks.

All eyes are on me, and I feel as if I'm the only person in the room who truly has no grasp of reality. I don't know what's going on. I don't even know if this is real or if I've somehow mentally cracked and am living some alternate reality. There's no way Christopher can be standing here in our house out in the middle of nowhere.

How did he find me?

Why would he even bother trying?

"Were you outside earlier, watching us?" I ask.

Confusion washes over his face. "No. I've been hiking all day, hoping to find you. Then I saw the smoke from the chimney and ran straight here. I hoped it was you. God, I'm so happy it is."

"How did you find us?"

"The same pilot who took you flew me here," he says. "And a shitload of luck."

"You risked your life—"

"Where is Richard?" Christopher asks, taking his snow-covered backpack off and spinning around the room some more.

"He and Scarecrow left to find us a new home," Holly answers for me. I'm grateful for her, since I can barely swallow my own spit, let alone speak in complete sentences. "They aren't here and won't be for quite some time."

And thank God for that. If they had been here, what would have happened? Someone would end up hurt, maybe dead. There is no way the meeting of the men would end good. I need to get Christopher out of here before they return, because the clash of the Titans would be devastating for all.

Christopher's eyes narrow on Holly. "And you are?"

Holly looks at Violet and then back at him. "We're Scarecrow's wives. We live here."

He takes a moment to analyze both women, who stand barefoot by the fire, wearing thin and worn floral dresses, and I wonder if he sees the old me in them. Does he see the ghost of Hallelujah Junction?

He subtly shakes his head, then closes the distance between him and me and finally takes me into his arms. Pressing my face into his chest, he holds me as if he never plans to let me go. "I was worried I would never see you again."

Wrapping my arms around his back and inhaling his spicy scent even through the wetness of his coat, I whisper back, "I never thought I'd see you again."

He presses his lips to the top of my head. "Why? Why did you leave?"

"I had to" is my only response.

"No, you didn't. You shouldn't have. You belong with me. We belong together."

I want to argue and explain why he's wrong, but I don't have the energy to fight the moment of euphoria I'm feeling from within the security of his arms.

"Ember?" I hear Violet's voice from behind me. "What's going on? Are you leaving?"

I break the hug and see a woman whose eyes are glistening and lip is trembling. I don't know how to answer her, because I don't know what's happening next.

Am I leaving?

Will I leave with Christopher?

Is it as simple as that? Or is it as difficult as that?

I don't know.

I don't know.

"I don't think *he* should be here," Violet adds. "If Scarecrow finds out about this...."

"No one's leaving right now," Holly says as she points to the side window revealing the snow, which is coming down harder and harder by the second. "It's a storm outside that is only going to get worse, and walking out that door will mean death."

Christopher reaches for his backpack and pulls out a large black phone. He presses some buttons and frowns at the screen. He then points it above his head and continues to scowl. "I need to get someplace not within the trees to get a better signal."

I instantly think of the cliff overlooking the canyon, but there's no way we can make our way there in this storm safely. "I know where we can go, but not until the snow stops."

He places the phone back in his bag and returns his attention to me. "Where exactly did Richard go?"

"Wyoming," I answer, feeling an odd sense of betrayal toward Papa Rich for telling of his whereabouts. "They're hoping they can find a small mining town like Hallelujah Junction that isn't so much on the radar as any place in Nevada or California right now."

"Scarecrow is going to be really angry when he finds out you're here," Violet says again, her voice cracking as she shifts her weight from one foot to the other.

I look at Violet and then Holly. I need a moment alone with Christopher without an audience. Luckily, Holly picks up on my need and discomfort.

She takes Violet by the hand and says, "Let's go over here and work on the chimney more. The snow's getting in and will snuff out our stew if we aren't careful."

I take this opportunity to take him to my corner of the chapel and pull the curtain to give us some visual privacy. I know that if Holly and Violet want to listen to our conversation, they can, but at least we have some seclusion. But no matter how much we whisper, the reality is that we are all in one room with no walls separating us.

"You shouldn't have come," I whisper, rubbing my arms to try to heat up my flesh that's gone cold.

"Did you really think I wouldn't?" He notices I'm cold and begins rubbing my arms for me, and though his hands are icicles themselves, they do offer a sense of warmth and comfort.

I don't know what I expected. But did I think Christopher would be able to track me down? Did I ever think I'd see him again?

No. Never in a million years.

"When the snow stops, we're getting out of here," he says.

I shake my head. "It's not that easy."

"It is. I have a satellite phone and a pilot on standby."

"Christopher... there's something you need to know." I want to throw up, and I sit down on my pallet of wool blankets, because if I don't sit, I'm afraid I'll collapse.

He sits down beside me, wraps his arm around my shoulders, and pulls me closer to his body. "We have shit to work out. But we can handle everything once we're in a safe place."

"When I left with Papa Rich and Scarecrow, I never thought I'd see you again," I begin.

"I'm your husband, Ember. I'm not going to just let you walk away that easily."

"But we aren't married. Not really. Your mother was right when she said that."

"Fuck my mother," he snaps. "I know what she did to you. I was fucking blind, and I should have paid closer attention, and for that I'm sorry. I'm so, so sorry you went through all of that alone."

I look up into his eyes. "You know about your mother finding Papa Rich?"

He nods as his jaw stiffens. "I know about everything. She was cruel to you, tried to fuck with your head and attempted to make you feel you were losing your mind. And though I'll never forgive her for what she did, I'm angrier with myself. I was so wrapped up in trying to get my life back. I wanted so desperately to have my normal to return. I kept telling myself that it was so I could care and provide for you, but that was total bullshit. I was being selfish and not focusing on you. I don't blame you one bit for leaving. I would have run for the hills too." He smirks and looks out the window at the falling snow. "Which you literally did."

"You were trying your best," I say. "And you deserved to have your life back. You had every right to want normal." I release a deep breath I've been holding. "Your mother told me that I was holding you captive. That I was just as guilty as Papa Rich in kidnapping you—"

"My mother is a selfish bitch. What she's done to you is criminal," he interrupts, his face reddening.

"But she was right in many ways. I *was* holding you captive. You didn't choose to marry me. It wasn't fair to expect you to remain married and take care of a woman and a situation you were forced into. You deserved better."

"I chose to stay with you," he growls. "Yes, our situation is not ideal. This isn't how I saw my life going, but regardless, the minute we left Hallelujah Junction, I knew I was committed to you. My wife. The woman I love." He reaches for my hand and squeezes it tightly. "And I still feel that way. I don't want you gone. I don't want us apart. I don't want my old life without you in it. I want *you*, Ember. I need you to understand that."

"But it's asking a lot. It's not fair to you. You should have been able to go back to your career without a worry in the world."

He nods again. "But it should have been something we did together. I was insensitive. I put me first. I know this, and I plan to fix it if you'll allow me to. I want us to leave here and start over. I want to be the husband you deserve."

Something is gripping my heart so tightly that I can barely breathe. I push myself away from Christopher and scurry a few feet away so I can have some room. I want to bury my nose in his chest and never face reality, but I also know I can't.

"I married Scarecrow," I blurt out.

I refuse to look at Christopher after I spit out the words, but I can hear his intake of breath.

"I don't understand."

I steal a glance at him and see the stunned confusion washed all over his face. I'm so ashamed for what I've done, how we got to this place, and for what's still ahead of me in the future. As happy as I am to see him again, I'm also devastated he has to see me in this light.

My true light.

"Papa Rich made me. He said that what happened between you and me was a mistake. That the devil made it happen, but that me marrying Scarecrow would correct the sin."

"This is insane."

"I didn't know what to do. I was so scared of what Papa Rich would do to me for burning down Hallelujah Junction. I felt like I was walking on eggshells, and... I left you. I left any chance, any hope, for a different life. My reality was right here." I point around. "This is my life. It's what my life has always been and what it will always be."

Christopher shoots up from sitting before me and towers over me. His eyes darken, and his entire presence morphs from a man offering me salvation to a man full of fury. "There is no way in hell I'm going to stand by and allow you to remain with that man. They are fucking lunatics who both deserve to be locked up for life. I don't care what they told you or what they forced you to do; there is no fucking way you're married to Scarecrow! Do you hear me?" His entire presence morphs to an almost beast-like creature. "I'll burn the fucking world down to keep you safe and next to me, starting with this place."

The sound of his booming voice rattles the rotting rafters above and dust speckles its way down on us.

"Ember?" I hear Holly call across the room. "Why don't you and Christopher come over here and join us by the fire? He's soaking wet, and it's cold."

"Did he fucking touch you? Did he... did he *make* you his wife?"

I shake my head vigorously, knowing exactly what he's asking. "He didn't consummate the marriage yet. He said he would when he returns." I swallow hard. "I haven't had sex with him."

He inhales deeply and appears relieved. He then looks out the window again. "We need to get out of here. Now."

"There's a blizzard coming," I say calmly. "We won't make it down the mountain. We may not be able to for days."

And that's if I go with him, which I can't see how it's truly possible.

He runs his hands through his hair and lets out a deep sigh.

"Ember," Holly calls out again. "Come sit by the fire and warm Christopher up until the stew is ready."

She's not going to give up, but she's skilled in knowing how to tame the beasts. She's had plenty of practice with Scarecrow.

"We should get you out of those wet clothes," I offer, knowing we need a break from all this for at least a moment.

I do.

I need to breathe. I need to focus. I need to stop the ringing in my ears.

He nods, but I can see he isn't happy.

I don't blame him.

I'm not happy either. But the difference between him and me is that happiness can be in his future. Not mine. I simply need to get him to face that hard fact.

I have. I've faced my dark future head-on. I've seen the red in the devil's eyes, and I've accepted his greeting.

11

EMBER

Christopher is restless in the chapel, and I don't blame him. I watch his eyes examine the girls and the way they're dressed. I know he has to hate seeing I reverted to my old look as well. He also seems to be looking for an escape route, as if he's expecting Papa Rich and Scarecrow to enter at any moment.

And that fact is a reality.

They could return.

They could hit weather of their own and decide they want to wait until winter has passed to start the journey to Wyoming. They may have also left us as a test. To see if we would indeed try to escape, regardless of how Holly feels that isn't true.

I can see them testing me. See if I'm trustworthy now after the Hallelujah Junction incident.

"How long have you lived here with Scarecrow?" he asks Holly and Violet.

"We don't really pay attention to days," Violet says softly. "Seasons are easier to track."

"Did he kidnap you too?" he asks.

"Our hands in marriage were promised by our father," Holly says, cutting more vegetables to throw in the stew. She knows we have another mouth to feed, and we barely cook enough for ourselves as it is.

"Your father married you off to *Scarecrow*?" Christopher says his name as if it burns his tongue.

Violet nods. "At least my sister and I could stay together."

"We need to get you both out of here too," Christopher declares as if it's as simple as that. "It's wrong what's been done to you."

Neither Holly nor Violet respond but look at me for answers.

Answers I don't have.

"We can't just leave," Holly finally says.

"Scarecrow would kill us if we did," Violet adds.

"Not if we go to a safe place," I suggest, realizing we really could all leave as one. "If the police get involved—"

"Weren't they already involved?" Holly asks. "And yet, you are here."

"You both don't need to be afraid of those men," Christopher reassures. "We'll get us all off this mountain, and I'll make sure that when they return... well, they won't like what's waiting for them."

Holly huffs. "You have no idea what you're up against. Scarecrow and Richard aren't going to simply walk into a trap. They're smart. Smarter than you give them credit for. Just because we all live off the grid doesn't mean we are inbred, uneducated fools."

I can see Holly is growing more and more agitated by the minute.

"I'm not saying you are," he says gently, most likely seeing her change in demeanor the same way as me.

"He wants to help," I tell her softly. "He only wants to help us."

"I'm going to go out and see if I can get a signal with the satellite phone," Christopher finally announces, not satisfied just sitting by the fire and maybe realizing there needs to be some space between him and the women.

I stand to go with him.

He puts out his hand and says, "I'll go alone. I'll only be a minute. No reason for you to get wet and cold."

He doesn't wait for me to argue but instead grabs his coat and hat hanging by the fire and heads out the front door.

Holly calls after him, "There's a cliff to the right. It's straight down to the canyon below. You may not be able to see well with the snow. I'd be careful not to get too close."

"I'll watch out," Christopher replies as he opens the door and charges into the harsh weather.

"If Scarecrow finds out about this...," Violet whispers as if someone can hear us.

"We'll be gone before he does," I say, though not with much confidence.

I'm just as scared as they must be. I've seen what happens when Scarecrow feels his wives have misbehaved. And sadly, it will be Violet—Wife Number Two—that will pay the price for us all.

I reach for Violet's trembling hand. "We'll be okay. I promise you. No matter what happens, we'll stick together and be okay."

Normally Violet likes my touch, but not now. Instead, she pulls her hand away sharply and shakes her head. "I'm going to get some firewood from the stables. I think we should before the snow buries us in."

I open my mouth to offer to help but then decide she needs the fresh air and the moment alone to process everything.

Or maybe that's what I need.

The front door opens and closes, and now it's just me and Holly. "We don't want to leave," Holly announces as she stirs the stew.

"I know the idea is scary—"

"We aren't like them," Holly adds quickly. "You know that, Ember. You lived out there and saw it for yourself."

"Christopher will help us."

"Even if we left with Christopher," Holly continues, "where would we go? What would we do? We have no money. We have no family other than Pa, who would beat us to death for leaving our husband and going against our vows to God. Leaving here is walking through the doors of hell."

I want to argue, but I don't have valid comebacks to what she's saying. She's right. We are different. Holly and Violet are no different from me. They were raised in captivity as I was, and being brought into the modern world is actually like walking into hell. They're right.

"You know you can't keep your sister with Scarecrow any longer. One day, he's going to beat her to death, and even if he doesn't... do you want your sister abused for the rest of her life? And what about you? I know you're forced to have sex with Scarecrow. You want to be raped forever?" My words come out harsher than I want, but I need Holly to start to see reason.

"We all have our paths in life."

"No," I snap. "That's what you were brought up to believe. You don't know any better. I didn't know any better, and though I didn't like New York... I liked it a hell of a lot more than I do this place. We all deserve better. We all deserve to truly be happy."

She smirks and shakes her head. "Happy is a fairy tale."

"I used to think that too. I still may. But I do know one thing. We can't be here when Scarecrow comes back. We can't be his three wives. It's no way to live."

She doesn't say anything but returns to the stew pot and begins stirring.

"Holly... I won't leave you and Violet."

"You may have to."

Christopher

The snow's coming down hard. So hard that walking in it is becoming more of a challenge as I sink into every step. I was warned to watch for the ledge, and with the falling snow, I can see how easily it could be for me to just walk right off.

Ember wanted to come with me, but I wanted her to stay warm, and I also got the sense that she needed some alone time with the sisters to explain what was going on. Plus, I don't want her standing in front of me if I do reach the authorities. I don't want her to actually hear me telling them where to arrest the man she still loves and sees as her father.

The wind is whipping around me, and though we aren't in blizzard conditions yet, we aren't far from it. I know we aren't getting off this mountain anytime soon, but I can at least reach out to the authorities and let them know Richard and Scarecrow are headed toward Wyoming, but more importantly... they will return here for the wives.

The wives.

The very thought of Scarecrow thinking Ember is *his* wife makes me ill and full of rage. If he even dared tried having sex with her... I would have cut off his other leg.

I still may.

"Please don't take her away from us," Violet says, walking up to me on the edge of the cliff as I search for a signal.

I turn to face her, surprised to see her outside without her sister or Ember. Something about her mousy and scared actions tells me this is out of her normal, to be so bold as to approach me.

"We can *all* leave," I say again, trying to reassure her that I meant it when I said we would all go together.

She shakes her head. "That's not what I mean. Even if Holly and I do go with you, I know Ember will be forever gone. With you. I'm asking you not to do that. I don't want to lose her. Please."

"You won't lose her," I assure. I can see the pain in her eyes as her lip trembles. "I see that Ember cares about you and your sister very much. We won't abandon you. I want to help you get a better life. A life that you deserve."

"I don't understand why you think leaving this mountain is a better life."

I glance down at the phone and see there is still no signal. I try to not show my frustration in the fact that I have to remain on the mountain another minute and give a fake smile. "It's better. Trust me."

I'm not giving her my full focus, and maybe I should, but at this moment in time, I'm standing on a cliff on a mountain in the middle of nowhere during a snowstorm that could last God knows how long.

"Did it ever cross your mind that maybe Holly and I wouldn't want to leave?"

I refocus on her, clearly seeing that she wants to have this conversation, and though it's damn cold outside, and we're getting soaked, she's determined.

Taking a calming breath and putting the phone away, I ask, "Why wouldn't you want to leave?"

"This is our home."

"With Scarecrow," I say with a snarl. Even the sound of his name and me having to say it makes me sick.

Her eyes glance down to the snow piling up around her booted feet. "He's our husband." She looks up at me. "And he's Ember's husband too."

Her words slap me in the face, and I clench my jaw not to shout obscenities back at her. "No. He's not."

She nods slowly, her eyes locked with mine. "But he is. You not liking that fact doesn't change the reality."

"Just because he made up vows, forced her to say them, and had some person claiming it so under God does not make it a legal wedding."

"Isn't that how you and Ember got married? So, are you saying she's not your wife too?"

This little pixie of a woman with her too-pale face and hollow eyes is pissing me off. I don't want to stand discussing this in the falling snow anymore.

I begin to walk back to the chapel. "We should get inside. It's really coming down, and we're going to get frostbite or hypothermia."

She reaches out and touches my arm as I try to pass her. She pauses, as if she's surprised she actually touched me—a man—but then she swallows back any uncertainty, straightens her shoulders, and stares back into my eyes.

"Do you want to know why Holly and I married Scarecrow?"

I don't say anything, but I remain standing in place.

"We married Scarecrow, because our pa deemed it so. But it wasn't a bad thing to get away from that situation—with our pa. Did we exchange one evil for the next? Maybe. But you know what? Holly and I welcomed the second evil."

"I'm sorry you had to do that," I say genuinely.

"Did you ever stop to wonder why Ember married Scarecrow?"

I don't answer but know exactly what she's going to say next.

"Because she welcomed the second evil."

I turn to walk toward the chapel, afraid what I may say next to the woman.

She takes a few quick steps so she can block my way. "And you want to bring her back and force her into the evil she was escaping. Is that fair? Is that truly what's best for Ember?"

My face heats regardless of the cold temperature. "Richard and Scarecrow deserve to be in prison. Period. End of discussion."

"And what do Holly, Ember, and I deserve?"

"Peace."

"Then don't take Ember away from us. Don't take her back to your world. *Your* world."

"We've been out here enough." I reach for her arm to assist her back into the house, but she pulls away from my touch as if I burned her skin.

She doesn't say another word but marches ahead of me back to the chapel.

Back to *her* world.

12

EMBER

Violet storms past me and walks over to the fire where Holly is, ignoring that I stand right by the door. She's upset, and it's the first time I've ever seen her this way.

"Holly," she snaps, "I think we should go get some wood from the barn. We need—" She looks over her shoulder at me. "—some space."

Christopher also walks into the chapel. He's taking deep breaths, and I know him well enough to know he's doing everything in his ability to not yell. We both step out of the way as Violet and Holly walk outside, and the coldness coming from them is far greater than the chill from the open door.

"She's right," I blurt to Christopher as he enters the chapel more. I heard the entire conversation between Violet and him.

"No, Ember. She's not right. She's scared. I understand that... or at least I'm trying to. I'm trying my best to understand what you are all feeling."

"But you don't, and you never will. That's the problem and will always be the problem. You and I come from two different worlds. We're different. And I don't see that fixing simply because you come up here and demand we all three leave with you."

He peers over his shoulder at me. My heart falls to the pit of my stomach at the hurt I see in his eyes.

"I want to be with you, but I can't just.... I hated New York." I pause and take a deep breath. "I wanted so badly to be the wife you deserve, but that place was swallowing me up whole. I felt trapped there. I felt like I was drowning in thick mud, and no matter how hard I tried to fit in... I didn't. I missed Hallelujah Junction. I missed my old life. I didn't want to tell you that, because I was scared you'd think I was crazy. I mean... maybe I am crazy. How could I possibly miss a place that held me captive? But I did."

"It's normal for you to miss what you've always known."

"It was more than that. It was more than the Stockholm Syndrome the therapist mentioned." I take another deep breath to drum up the courage to finally tell the entire truth. "I fantasized about you and me back in the schoolhouse. I missed our chain around our ankles. I missed the time it was just you and me... connected. I liked that we shared the same air as we took each breath. I liked that I had to walk with you in cadence as the metal jangled around our feet. I missed the warmth I felt from your body at all times because there was never any space. I missed our captivity. I missed you," I confess, unconsciously reaching out a hand, beckoning his touch.

He stares at my hand and then at my tear-filled eyes. His expression is firm, unbreakable, then softly it melts. He turns so he faces me fully, his body taking up the entire space of the doorway.

I stand still, barely breathing, my hand still outstretched. "I do want you. I want it more than anything. I just don't know how to want all that comes with you."

"Do you really feel we can't fix this? Do you think we can't be together simply because of New York? Because I'm here to tell you that we can fix anything."

The weight of my past feels like a hundred-pound brick rests on each shoulder. "I don't know how to be normal. I tried. I hope you saw how much I truly tried. I wore the clothes. The shoes. I tried to go to the parties."

He simply nods.

"When I was growing up, reading every romance book I could get my hands on, I would dream of the day I'd find my own Prince Charming and go to the fancy parties and live in the large house with lavish furniture and chandeliers in every room. And then all of a sudden, I had it. I had it all. But what it really became was a deep, deep hole that I sank into."

"So, we don't go back to the house. I should have found our own place right at the beginning," he says. "And if you hate New York, then we'll move someplace else. Maybe a small town with less noise and action."

"And what about you? That's your home. That's who *you* are. I can't pull you away from everything you've ever known any more than you can pull me away from what I have grown up with. We are who we are."

"And you think we need to do that apart? Be who we are?"

I tense, fighting the devastation that threatens to consume me. I search his face, his posture, for some clue as to what he feels. "Yes," I barely whisper.

"You're wrong." Christopher takes the few steps that separates us and grabs my hand. "You and I have one thing that is stronger than all else. Love."

Tears well in my eyes; pain wells in my heart. "We are the demented love story. Remember?"

He pulls me into his arms, burying my face against his chest. "But a love story, nonetheless. I love you, Ember. I know that with every inch of my being. I also know I can't live without you. So, yes, if we *both* have to start over so we can begin anew, then so be it. The question is if you are willing to."

I nod against his warmth. "I want to. I want to so badly. I'm just scared. And I love you. I love you so much that it actually hurts when I think about it. My chest tightens to the point of pain."

"Then we fight," he murmurs against my hair. "We fight against every single person getting in our way. No one will block us any longer. No one and nothing. You are *my bride*, and I'm taking you back."

"How? There's still a storm outside, and based on what Holly says, it could keep going for days," I counter, clutching tighter to him. "And I know you said we'd call the police on Richard and Scarecrow. But then where does that leave Holly and Violet?"

"We'll figure it all out." He looks out the door at the snow falling and then closes it behind him. I realize the door has remained open the entire time. Maybe giving us both the option to flee. A choice we've both decided against.

He then tips my face up to meet his, his eyes filled with a blend of love and passion. "I love you."

"I love you."

I turn to walk away and put some logs on the fire, knowing Holly and Violet will be back with a fresh pile of firewood soon. Christopher grabs hold of my wrist and pulls me close to him. He leads us to my private corner with nothing but a tattered sheet, concealing what I know is coming next.

"Not yet," he says. "Don't walk away yet."

"But the fire... I should tend to the fire." I turn away again, but he pulls me harder.

I look over my shoulder, down at my wrist that is firmly gripped, and then back into his eyes.

He tugs my arm toward him, giving me no choice but to stumble up against his chest.

"Kiss me," he orders in a gruff whisper.

I follow his direction gladly. I want nothing more than to feel his lips against mine.

Our mouths meet, a pull neither can resist any longer. Our hunger demands to be satiated. Time and distance has kept us apart, but our true love never broke. His heart beats against mine as he arranges my body closer. The single kiss has the power to reunite us forever, forgetting all the wrong by both. The kiss is the period to our run-on sentence that seems to never end. One kiss speaks volumes for what is meant.

I want him.

I want him this very second... regardless of our current location and situation. Regardless that Holly and Violet can enter the chapel at any minute. And regardless that I don't know if we will ever get our happily ever after. But I want him...

Now.

"I need to be with my wife," he says as his eyes seem to darken right before me.

My heart skips, knowing he feels the same way I do. Our bodies are in tune, even though our lives will never be.

Without asking, without pausing, he removes my dress effortlessly, nothing beneath it to cover me. I'm completely naked, standing before my husband.

"I need you too, but...." I can feel the heat of his stare on my naked body, but I don't try to conceal myself. I stand and await his next command.

"Don't fight this. Stop fighting us."

He leans forward, takes hold of my hips, and pulls me closer to him. Kiss by kiss, he lowers us to the makeshift bed, and then lowers further down until his face is inches from my sex.

"I want the taste of you on my tongue." He doesn't wait for permission but rather kisses my pussy, followed by licking my throbbing clit.

I tense at the invasion—thinking I'd never get to feel such pleasure ever again in my life. Part of me wants to stop, and the other part wants the feeling to never end.

He swirls his tongue in circles, lapping up every sign of my arousal. I moan with complete abandon, knowing Holly and Violet could walk in at any minute, but I can't resist.

My body seems possessed by Satan himself—no doubt something Papa Rich would accuse me of. I have absolutely no power against the devil when it comes to what Christopher is able to do to my body.

Lick after lick, he brings my body to another level. Just when I believe I can take no more, he thrusts his finger past the lips of my pussy. In and out, he plunges, pulling gasps and muffled moans from me. I hide my face beneath a pillow in hopes of concealing my rising pleasure.

"Spread your legs wider," he directs, his voice husky.

Suffocated by love at the familiar—yet so very distant memory—command, I do exactly as he asks without any hesitation. Lying beneath his shadow, I peek up from the pillow to see his face. The strong features, the firm lips, the sensitive eyes. The same expression I remember washes over his face... strength, love, passion. These are the eyes of my husband. The man I vowed to love. The man I vowed to spend the rest of my life with.

And yet... I ran.

I broke the vows.

I shattered everything.

"I'm sorry," I murmur more to myself than to him. "I'm so sorry I left."

"Shh," he whispers as he places his lips to my pussy.

His intimate kiss forgives, but does he?

His body is offering amnesty, but does his heart?

He caresses my mound without saying a word, quickly following with a kiss to my belly and then my slit. Once. Twice. The kissing continues as heat ripples over my body in waves, leaving me breathless. "Christopher," I whisper. "I—"

I want to apologize over and over if this is my penance.

Further words are lost as his kisses turn into licks and nibbles. The sting of his bites on my inner thigh makes me want to beg for mercy yet also leaves me wanting more. Moaning, gasping, whimpering, I close my eyes and give myself up to the moment... to Christopher and his show of forgiveness.

He pauses a moment, rubbing his hand along my heated flesh. Dipping his finger down the crease of my butt, he presses past and rests his finger at the entrance of my tight rosebud, teasing me with the unknown of what's to come. Slight pressure is added, but not enough to break past and enter fully. Slowly, he lowers his other hand to my silky folds, wet with desire.

A deep moan rumbles in his chest and escapes as he thrusts his finger into my hungry sex. I buck against his hand, moaning in pleasure. Dizzy with the need for more, I do everything I can not to beg to be fucked right then and there.

I don't want Holly and Violet to hear from outside, but at the same time, my body doesn't care. I need Christopher. I need him now, and my body and soul nearly scream out in desire.

His finger is soon followed by a second as he pumps in and out of me, demanding my complete surrender to his touch. Trying my best to remain quiet but failing miserably, I can do nothing more but allow the climax to build. And when he removes his slick finger and presses it into my anus without warning, the orgasm rocks my body at an intensity that has me screaming out.

Submission, passion, and animalistic need for more explodes through my body like the crack of lightning during a desert thunderstorm. Moaning, I press against his hand, driving his finger deeper into my forbidden channel, his touch entrenched within me as I melt against him.

With one finger buried in the taboo, he places the palm of his other hand on my wet and needy pussy, continuing on with the stroking and caressing. One, two, three fingers are pushed inside my pussy, and I mewl as the erotic bite sends me to the edge once again. My breath catches in my throat as I hold back a cry of lustful yearning. I can't focus, lost in a fog of bliss. Pleasure and pain weave themselves together, escalating until I cry out his name in a husky whisper that doesn't sound like my own voice.

After the final orgasmic wave leaves my body, he cups his hand over my pussy, using it to adjust my body until I'm tucked snuggly into his arms. Instinctively, I nuzzle my face against the warmth of his neck, and my body melts to his. The feelings, the emotions... nothing can describe them.

Other than safe.

I'm safe with Christopher.

It's the only time in my life I truly feel this way.

Safe.

"Tell me that you'll never leave me again," he whispers into my hair as he follows the command with a kiss to my head.

I pause, because I don't want to promise things I can't keep. I don't know what happens next. I don't know if I can do what he wants.

Can I simply leave?

Can I walk away from Holly and Violet?

Can I go back to the life in which I didn't belong?

Instead of saying what he wants to hear, I pull away enough so I can kiss him.

The only thing I can promise right now is to always love him. That much will always be true.

"I love you, Christopher. I love you so much."

I kiss him again, driving my tongue into his mouth, hoping my answer will do for now.

13

EMBER

I've wanted this.

I've lied to myself, pretending that I didn't.

I want Christopher.

I've always wanted Christopher.

And now that I have him, I'm never letting him go.

"Take off your clothes," I say, my strong coming back.

I feared I lost this part of me. The strong woman who asks for what she wants.

He does as I demand, his eyes locked with mine the entire time. He then slips his hand around my waist, repositioning us so he's on top of me fully. Fingers laced, thighs rubbing against thighs, my breasts molded to his torso, his cock resting at my entrance—heavy and hot.

Not wasting another moment, he moves to kneel before my face and places his hard dick to my lips. I look up and into his eyes. No words need to be said. I open up my mouth and allow his cock to lie against my tongue. My natural instinct is to pleasure him. It's always been the one thing I want to do to him more than anything else.

Pleasure him.

I'm good at this.

I thrive at this.

I'm proud that I can do this so well.

Watching bliss blanket his face fills me with a purpose I didn't know existed before I met this man, and I wonder if I will ever get to experience it again in my lifetime if indeed Christopher and I have to part ways. As I suck up and down his ready dick, I fully submit to an old hope for the future that now renews.

Maybe... just maybe... we can have a happily ever after.

Maybe he can rescue me from this mountain, and we can have it all.

Maybe I can truly be free and not captured in Papa Rich's web.

Maybe... just maybe.

Up and down, I move my mouth until I'm rewarded by my name escaping his lips in the most passionate of ways. My name never sounded as good as it does the moment it slips from his mouth.

I add my hand and begin to pump his cock while licking all around it. His body shakes and tenses, and he pulls me away as he takes a deep breath.

"I've missed your kiss," he says, his gaze dipping to my lips. "I've missed everything about you and what you do to me. But mostly, I miss the way you make me feel. I was so scared I'd never be able to tell you this. I was so scared we'd never be like this again."

His moment of vulnerability only spurs me on. I need it. I need it to regain my strength, to take hold of my confidence, to return to the Ember I was working so hard to be.

Reflexively, I slip my tongue across my mouth, waiting for his to make contact.

Slowly, he pulls me up to him.

We kiss, soft, romantic, and pure.

Husband and wife blocking out all the bad around us.

He slides his hand to the wetness of my sex, driving my thirst for him to be inside me to a whole new level. I approach the edge, wanting desperately for more. "Please, Christopher. I need you."

Christopher cups my face and plants a slow, deep kiss on my lips. His mouth blazes a path from my lips to the base of my neck. I let a sensual moan escape regardless of how quiet I've been trying to be, hoping to encourage him to keep going.

Skimming my fingers down his rippled stomach, I simply moan and wait. I know he'll give me exactly what I want if I just wait. I can count on him. I can rely on him. Always.

"You're mine, Ember. Mine forever, no matter who tries to get in the way of that."

I gasp at the sensation of his cock pressing against me at the end of his declaration.

Closing my eyes in ecstasy, I dig my fingers into his shoulders as he presses beyond the tightness, entering me completely. The delicious sting is quickly replaced with an erotic pleasure that captures my breath.

He continues to place gentle kisses all over my neck and face while his thick shaft probes deeper within. The contrast of soft and hard manages to push me toward that familiar edge. Sparks, electricity, pure primal need washes over me, drowning me in pleasure as we both rock each other into completion.

There is nothing else but us.

Christopher and Ember.

I don't know how long we lie there, but I take the time of silence to focus on his breathing and the beating of his heart. I touch the tiny curls on his chest and trace my fingertip over the ridges of his stomach. I'm hypnotized by the feeling of contentment and security, but I also know we can't stay in this little euphoric bubble forever.

"I've missed you so much, Ember. I've missed the feel of you in my arms," Christopher murmurs into my hair.

"I missed you too. More than I thought possible." I smile at him as I pull away from his warm embrace, and I put on the last of my clothing, wishing we could be naked in each other's arms forever. But I have Holly and Violet to think about. Not to mention the storm is still raging outside, and the biting wind is forcing its way inside the chapel. They'll be back from the barn soon simply because they will have no choice.

"I want us to leave the minute this storm allows," he says, the determination in his eyes as unrelenting as the tone of his voice. It's clear the reality of our situation has hit him again, and his moment of sex-induced amnesia is gone. "I want you back in my life, and I want us to forget this place and any future places Richard offers."

When I open my mouth to protest, Christopher cuts me off. "And I don't give a fuck what wedding vows Scarecrow made you say, or the fact that they think you are now his wife. No fucking way. Do you hear me?"

"It's just…"

I look at the pulled curtain offering us the limited privacy we needed—faded and worn—knowing what's on the other side.

My new life.

A life that now involves other people. Though I have just met them in actual days, if feels like a lifetime. They get me, I get them. We walk the same path in life and always have. When I look at them, it's like looking in a mirror.

"It's not that simple," I finally say.

"Yes, it is," Christopher says, sitting up and reaching for his shirt. "This isn't open for discussion, Ember. I don't want to be an asshole, but I will if I have to be. We're leaving this place, and it's final." He then stands and puts on his pants. "I get it. We have shit to work out, but we'll work it out together. I'm going to get you as far away from this madness, and I'm never going to let you come this close to those sick fuckers again."

"Except this 'madness' also includes two women who I've become close to. I can't just leave them here. And I get the feeling they are determined to stay."

"Then we'll allow them to do what they want. But *you* will not stay. Period."

"I can't leave without them. It's not an option. What do you think Papa Rich and Scarecrow will do to them when they return and find me gone?"

"What Richard and Scarecrow will come home to find is the police waiting to arrest their asses."

I sigh deeply. "You say that. But the police haven't exactly been much help since the day we left Hallelujah Junction. I don't really have faith in them."

The truth of the matter is I don't really have faith in anyone. Which I suppose is sad. Funny how I saw life in such a happier way when I was being told lies and mentally being held captive in a schoolhouse in a ghost town with a serial killer as a "father."

Maybe Louisa was right about me—I'm broken. Just a freak. And the reality is... I belong here with Holly and Violet. They get me. They *are* me in a sick and twisted way.

"Ember...."

I lean forward and give him a quick, avoiding-the-topic peck. "I hear footsteps in the snow outside. Holly and Violet are here."

14

CHRISTOPHER

It's been twenty-four hours since I arrived, and I'm going freaking crazy. Cabin fever is truly a real thing. The snow is falling softer now, but it dumped overnight and most of the day, and I'm not sure how easy hiking down the mountain is going to be for any of us. The women don't have warm clothing, or at least not warm enough. They go out into the elements to collect wood with nothing but crocheted shawls over their thin dresses that hang off their narrow shoulders. At least they all seem to have rainboots to slip on and off when they do go out, but even those may not be good enough if we are sinking to our knees with every step.

Holly and Violet also seem to be malnourished, and though their strength and energy seem to be up, I still worry if they will have the stamina it will take to make it to the makeshift tarmac in the valley I was dropped off on.

The other concern I have is their respiratory system. Both women have a hack when they cough. Neither seems sick, but after staying in the chapel for one night, I clearly see the culprit. The fire is releasing too much smoke in the chapel. Though they have worked on a chimney of sorts, it's neither completed nor all that effective. It's blocking the snow from extinguishing the flames, but the amount of smoke now being trapped inside is downright dangerous. And based on their coughs... this is something they have been dealing with for a while.

Violet stands from where she's been sitting and staring at the fire in silence for the entire day. "I'm going to get us some more wood."

The rate we've been burning the wood to keep warm is keeping us up all hours and having to recollect to stoke the fire. And it's going to be another cold one tonight.

"I'll go," I offer, needing to get up and stretch my legs anyway. Plus, my eyes are starting to burn from all the smoke.

She pauses, nods, then sits and stares at the fire some more. She has barely spoken since her conversation with me near the cliff. It's very clear I am not one of her favorite people, and though I feel for her situation and am trying to be sensitive to her feelings, I will pick her up and carry her down the mountain if I have to if it means Ember agreeing to leave with me.

Ember has agreed, but I see her wavering. I think it depends on the moment for her. One second, she wants to run away with me this instant, but the next minute, she wants to stay with the sisters and feels obligated to keep them happy with whatever they need.

I'm scared that the longer we stay, the harder it will be to convince any of them to leave.

I walk over to Ember, who is peeling some potatoes, and kiss the top of her head. She stops to look at me. "Do you want some help?"

"I'm fine. It's too cold for any of you to be out there without the proper clothing," I say, reaching for my coat and hat hanging by the fire. "I'll be right back."

I need to check out the path I took up here to see if it's even possible for us to leave anytime soon. I also reach for my satellite phone again in hopes that maybe, just maybe, I can get a signal.

I'm right in worrying about us sinking to our knees in snow, because the minute I walk out of the chapel, that is exactly what I do. I suppose it could be worse—it could be to our thighs.

Trekking through the snow, I walk all around the area with my arm up, hoping I can catch a signal if I just turn the right way. The snow has stopped falling for the time being, and the evening sky is peeking out from the clouds. Maybe it will warm up some, and the snow will start to melt tomorrow. I can't even see where I hiked up, so I'd have to carve a new path for us, which I'm prepared to do.

Giving up on the phone, I pocket it and head toward the barn that is holding the firewood. When I make my way in that direction, I hear a rustling in the dense forest to my left. I freeze, wishing I had brought a weapon with me so I could hunt whatever animal is nearby. But when I steal a glance, I swear it's not an animal I see. It's human.

Whoever it is quickly scurries away, but I know without a doubt it isn't a deer or a bobcat or any other woodland creature.

It's them.

It has to be them.

They are watching. Waiting. Planning.

I run toward the edge of the forest, not truly thinking my actions through. I have absolutely nothing to defend myself with, but if it's Richard or Scarecrow, I'll kill them with my bare hands if I have to.

"Richard!" I shout toward the forest. "You fucking coward. Come out and face me! I know it's you. Scarecrow? Can you hear me? I'm here with your wives! They're mine now. Mine. Do you hear me? How does that make you feel? Get your one-legged shithead self out here and fight for what's yours!"

Silence.

"Fucking cowards!"

Silence.

I run toward the exact location I saw the movement and don't see any footsteps in the snow. But I do see disruption. They're covering their tracks behind them as they run away. I know I can follow the tracks... and I may, but first I need to get back to the chapel and prepare the women. I also need to grab my gun that I packed. I didn't plan on using it unless necessary, but if those assholes are here... it's necessary.

Ember must have heard me shouting, because she comes running out of the chapel, wide-eyed and calling my name.

"Go back inside," I say as I run toward her.

She doesn't do as I ask until I reach her, but we both run inside together as I slam the door behind me.

"Richard and Scarecrow are here. They're in the forest," I say, winded from my run in the deep snow.

Holly and Violet both stand up quickly, panic on their faces.

"What? You saw them?" Ember asks, her hand over her mouth, terror in her eyes.

"No," I say. "I didn't get a good look, but I know there was someone."

Holly and Violet look at each other and then back at me. "It could be an animal," Holly suggests.

I charge toward my pack and pull out my gun, turning off the safety and preparing to use it. "It was a man. I know it was."

"I swear I saw someone watching us too," Ember says. "I worried it was them as well."

"It just doesn't make sense," Violet says. "If it's Richard and Scarecrow, why wouldn't they come inside? Why would they stay in the woods with no shelter? Especially all night in a storm."

"Because they're insane! They're sick motherfuckers with no rhyme or reason to what they do!" My voice booms throughout the chapel, and I realize I'm losing control.

I have to keep my control and wits about me to defeat them. I can't let them get inside my head so that I make poor decisions. They're playing a game of cat and mouse, but this time the mouse will tear the cat to shreds.

Violet runs to the window by the door and peers out. "I don't see anything."

Ember joins her to look. "I don't think you should go out there. What if that's what they want you to do? They might have guns too."

"If they wanted to shoot me, they had the opportunity," I say, marching to the door. "And if they were wise men, they would have. I'm not going to be afraid of those men and hide in this chapel. If they want a fight, I'm ready to give it to them."

I run back toward the forest's edge. My trek is easier this time with the adrenaline as well as running back across packed snow from where I was before. I run into the forest and follow the trail for as far as I can. I'm getting farther and farther into the thickness of the trees until I reach a creek, and then just like that, the trail is gone. I can't tell where they went.

Gone.

The motherfuckers are gone.

I spin around and call out, "Are you watching me? Get a good look, fuckers. Look at the man who is going to bring you down. You can hide like the rats you are. But I'll find you. I'll find you!"

My voice bounces off the trees and seems to echo back at me.

Complete silence after that.

I don't even hear a chirp of a bird.

"Christopher! Christopher!" I hear Ember's voice calling from up near our shelter.

I know she's got to be terrified, so without wasting another second taunting men who may or not be within earshot, I run back toward her.

When I see her, she appears frantic as she trudges through the snow toward me.

"They're gone," I say as I approach and take her into my arms.

She glances around me at the forest. "I swear I saw them too." She's winded from her run. "But why? It makes no sense that they'd stay out there. They could freeze to death."

"I don't know," I reply as I lead her back to the warmth of the chapel. "But we need to get out of here as soon as we can. They're planning something. I'm not going to just sit here and allow them to hunt us like prey."

"Did you see anything?" Violet asks as we enter.

I shake my head. "They ran off."

"How do you know it wasn't an animal? We're surrounded by them here."

"I just know," I answer.

"I agree with Christopher," Ember says. "I still feel like I saw someone as well. My gut tells me it isn't an animal out there."

"You both don't know this mountain," Holly says. "We do."

"And we know what is and what isn't out there," Violet adds.

They both look at each other, which sends alarm bells off inside me. It's the second time they've given a knowing look to each other.

"What the fuck aren't you telling us?" I ask firmly. "I can tell there's something."

Holly snaps her head toward Christopher as if prepared for an attack. "Excuse me?"

"I've seen you both looking at each other," I say.

"I've felt like you may be keeping something from me as well," Ember confesses. "You were quick to tell me what I saw was also an animal."

"We just know Scarecrow wouldn't stay out there. He doesn't like to be uncomfortable. He wouldn't allow us to be sitting by the fire while he's out in the cold," Violet cuts in.

She has a point, and it truly doesn't make sense how Richard and Scarecrow could have survived last night in the snow. But maybe there is a hunting shack they know of and are hiding there. Regardless of their reasons, their thinking, or their sick plans, I know what I saw, I know what I feel, and I know there was a man watching. Not an animal, but a man.

And though I'm not going to push the issue anymore for right now, I also feel that Holly and Violet know something and are keeping it secret.

Holly hasn't stopped glaring at me, and Violet is biting her nails so hard there may be nothing left when she's done. I'm not going to apologize for my actions or my beliefs, and if I have to stand here watching them all day to get some answers, then I will. Eventually I'll be able to read them and figure out what's going on.

Ember must be picking up on the tension in the room, because she suggests, "It's getting dark. Why don't we settle in for the night, eat some potato soup I made, and go to sleep early."

"You never got the firewood," Violet says with a scowl. "I'll go get it."

I consider stopping her to go get it myself, but Holly adds, "I'll help. We can chop some wood while we're out there."

Frankly, right now, I need them out of the chapel. I need a minute to breathe. I need a minute with Ember. And I need a minute to just process the madness that is presented before me.

15

Ember

"They're just scared," I try to defend. "Holly and Violet live a life that no one can understand."

"I know," he says. "I don't understand. Just as I didn't truly understand all you were struggling with. I won't make the mistake of thinking I do again."

"But they are keeping something from us," I concede.

"They are," he agrees. "But I'm not going to push anymore. I'm just going to watch and keep my eyes open."

"They wouldn't hurt us," I say, truly believing the words.

"I believe that. I don't think it's in their nature to hurt anyone. But I also think they will do whatever Scarecrow tells them. They will also do whatever they can to survive. If lying to you and me about a bigger plan is what it takes for survival, I don't think they'll have a choice."

"I'm so sorry," I murmur as I place my hand gently on Christopher's shoulder. "You're here because of me, and I'm sorry."

"We both have things to be sorry for," he says, releasing the breath he seemed to be holding. "But I wouldn't want to be anywhere else without you. This is temporary, and we will get out of here. Regardless of whether Richard and Scarecrow are out there or not, we're leaving tomorrow if the snow lets up. We'll let the authorities deal with them."

"Do you think they'll come tonight?"

He holds up his gun. "I hope they fucking do. I'd like to end this right now."

"You aren't a ruthless killer," I say as my heart skips at the idea of him doing something so violent as to kill another human being. I know he wanted Papa

Rich to burn in Hallelujah Junction, but setting a fire and running away is a far cry different than staring a man straight in the eye and then pulling the trigger.

"Just like Holly and Violet, I'll do whatever it takes to survive and to protect you."

My eyes go to the gun, to his dark eyes and tight jaw, and then back to the gun. "This wouldn't have happened if I didn't leave. I put us in danger. It's all my fault."

He clicks the safety on the gun, puts it on the table, and takes me into his arms. "Let's focus on the future and stop beating ourselves up for what we did or didn't do in the past. There's no need to keep punishing ourselves." He kisses the top of my head. "I think we've both gone through enough for one lifetime. This will all be a distant memory soon enough. When we leave here, it will just be you and me. We'll block out all the bad, all the resistance, and anything and anyone who is trying to keep us apart. I promise you, Ember. It'll be better. I swear."

I pull away just enough so that I can kiss him. I need his affection more than I've ever needed anything. I need his taste. I need his smell. I need him.

"I should have trusted in your love for me," I whisper through our kiss.

"Yes, you should have," he says and then kisses me deeper.

We should wait. We shouldn't be doing this here. Not here.

We have an entire life to do this.

A new home to create, where we can be together over and over again, in the privacy of our own space, but I just can't get enough of this man. And with how much he's constantly touching me, kissing me, and giving me the hungry look that makes my knees nearly melt... he can't get enough of me either.

We try to be discreet, but the sisters know.

And I feel guilty for it. Maybe because I'm getting happiness and love when they aren't.

Or maybe...

As sick as it sounds, I may feel guilty because deep down I worry they are judging me for committing adultery on Scarecrow. Maybe they don't understand that Christopher is my husband in all ways that matter and always has been. Maybe they think what I'm doing is wrong. Dirty. Sinful.

Yes, I fear the sisters think I'm a sinner.

And I do care what they think. I desperately want them to approve of me and Christopher. I want them to see in him what I see. I want them to trust him when he tells them he will keep them safe. I want them to believe when he says he will help them start over and have a better life. I want them to have faith that all will be well, and we can all be a family... in our own demented way.

But I don't think they do.

They watch. They're quiet. They go about the hours that pass in a silence that makes me uneasy. Violet seems hurt. Almost as if I've betrayed her by allowing Christopher to reach out and hold my hand.

I wish I could make it all better.

I wish I could make *them* better.

I also wish I could resist Christopher right now... but I can't.

He doesn't hesitate, and I'm thankful when he guides us to my private nook, shedding me of my dress as he does. If the sisters enter, at least we won't be in plain sight, but I still hope they stew outside in the barn for a little longer.

He lowers me to our poor excuse of a bed, but I've never been happier to make contact with the rough wool.

I know what's coming next.

Christopher sucks my breast, then moves to the other to give it equal attention. Lowering his hand to my mound, damp with fresh arousal, he dips a finger to my clit and applies pressure as he rouses an overwhelming longing that has me gasping for air.

Moving from my clit, he presses his fingers past my silky folds and pushes one, then two digits into my sex. I force my hips up to drive them inside my pussy even deeper.

They aren't enough.

I want to feel the small bite of pain as his cock stretches me while he claims what is now his. I want to feel him so badly that the hunger changes who I am.

I'm not Ember—the timid, scared, and broken woman.

I'm an animal.

Primal.

I'm a stalker in search of its victim.

I'm a woman who needs to be fucked hard by her man. Her man who nearly slipped away but now will forever be in her grips.

This is me. Powerful, knowing, willing to fight for what I want.

I want Christopher.

I want to be married to him and spend the rest of my life with him.

But right now...

Right now, I want his cock, and I'm not ashamed to admit it. It's natural, it's right, and there isn't anything sinful about my needs and desires. I'm learning this. I'm growing, and as I do, I will take what's mine. Mine.

Christopher is mine.

Unable to hold back the fever that scorches me, I beg, "Please, Christopher. Please..."

"Please what?" he teases as he dances his fingers inside my core. "Say it, Ember. Tell me what you want. I want to hear the dirty words come from this perfect mouth." He nibbles on my bottom lip and then pulls away, staring into my eyes.

I want to look away, because the familiar timid girl still lurks inside me, but his eyes demand that I keep them in place. My body obeys. My mind obeys. I obey.

"I want you," I pant, desperately wanting to feel the orgasm that rests just beneath the surface, begging to be set free. But I need my husband's heavy dick spreading me to make that happen.

"Not dirty enough." He pulls his fingers out of my pussy as punishment.

"Fuck me!" I blurt out as a moan follows my frantic command. "I want you to fuck me hard and make me feel you between my legs tomorrow. I want it to be rough. I want it to sting. I want to feel the pain that is followed by pleasure. I want your cock to stretch me and fill me. Fuck me!"

I am absolutely thirsty and ravenous at this point as his fingers hit a spot inside my pussy that has me uncontrollably twirling in ecstasy. There isn't anything I wouldn't do to have him enter me deep and hard. The power this man has over me....

Sparing me of my uncontrollable desires, he finally grants me my filthy wish. He sheds his clothes as fast as possible and mounts me. Feeling his weight on top of me, I'm soon rewarded as his cock presses up against my opening and easily slides in with the aid of my soaking wet pussy. Wrapping my legs around him, I hold on in fear that he'll change his mind and torture me some more.

And with a forceful shove of his hips, he drives his thick cock all the way in, claiming me completely. So deep. So fucking deep.

I want to stay like this always. Connected. Always connected.

Yes, yes, yes... I am his. I should have never left. I should have never allowed anyone or anything to get in the way. I should have resisted the voices in my head that tried to take over. I should have run away from the darkness and only looked toward the light.

Christopher—my light.

In and out, he thrusts, deeper and deeper with each pounding action. My moans blend with his as our bodies merge as one—as *only* one, like we are meant to be. Fate—she has brought us together more than once, and it's about time I fucking listen to her.

"This pussy of yours is mine. Only mine," he growls as he powers into me, his muscles taut, his eyes glazed over with a fierce intensity that only drives me closer to the edge. "I want to hear you moan my name," he demands. "Moan."

As if I can do nothing else but obey, I do just as he orders.

Moaning with each vibration of wantonness that attacks my pussy, I truly collapse into an encompassing hole of sexual bliss.

With a few more thrusts, Christopher's groans blend with the sounds of my completion, and he too joins me in our own world of lust.

Slipping my arms around his neck, I pull away enough to stare into his eyes. "I'll never run away from you—from us—again." Choked by emotion, I rest my head on his shoulder and close my eyes, wishing the moment of connection could last forever.

"I should've never given you reason to leave," he murmurs, drawing my lips to his. "You're everything—" But before he can say more, the door to the chapel opens, and the sound of booted feet breaks our privacy.

"Ember? Christopher?" Holly calls out.

We both stand and scurry for our clothing, dressing as fast as we can. I don't think they will move the curtain, but maybe they will.

Scanning each other quickly to make sure we're appropriately dressed, we both walk out from the curtain to greet the sisters.

Caught in the act, but an act I hope to do again, and again, and again, I wonder if I'll ever get enough of this man.

16

EMBER

We're all sitting around the fire in silence, eating leftover soup from last night. It's awkward. We've been coexisting in a suffocating tension that I can barely stand. I look at Christopher with pleading eyes. I want this to be better. It has to get better.

Christopher must read my mind, because he clears his throat and says, "I'd like to apologize for my aggression last night. I really feel as if Richard and Scarecrow are out there, but regardless if they are, I feel I may have scared you with how I acted. I'm also sorry for accusing you both of keeping something from us."

Holly looks up from her soup and gives him a small smile. "It's a stressful time," she offers. "We understand."

Violets shoots daggers at Holly, clearly not appreciating having her sister speak for her.

"I know the topic of us all leaving is a sensitive one, but it's still one we need to discuss," Christopher continues, putting down his bowl. "The storm has passed, and I feel like we have a very small window to act. We need to get down the mountain to where I can reach a pilot to fly us out of here. We need him to reach us before he can't due to more weather."

I look at Holly and Violet. "Please come with us," I beg. "I know you're scared. I am too. But we'll get through this together."

"No," Violet says. "My answer is no." She gets up without another word and storms out of the chapel.

"We need a little more time," Holly says, grabbing all our empty bowls and bringing them to a large barrel we use for dishes. "Just give her time."

"I'm going to go check on her," I say, getting up, feeling like I need to.

"Do you want me to go with you?" Christopher asks.

"I'll be right back. I need to talk to her in private," I reply.

I walk outside, happy to see the sun is out and the snow is indeed melting as Christopher was hoping it would do. I walk to the barn, which is the only form of real shelter other than the chapel on this property. When I don't find Violet inside, I walk out and see her standing outside near the cliff.

"Violet? What are you doing out here?" I ask as I approach her. The snow has stopped falling, but the temperatures are still near freezing, and being close to the cliff isn't safe at any time, but definitely not now.

She doesn't turn to face me but instead looks out over the canyon. The clouds hang low, and all the treetops are covered in white.

"Did you convince Holly to go with you?" she asks softly. If the air wasn't so eerily still, I'm not sure I'd hear her.

"She hasn't decided yet."

"But you have?"

"I have. I'm leaving with Christopher. I love him."

I take a step toward her, noticing she's dangerously close to the ledge. "Violet, why don't you step away from the edge. It's icy. I don't want you slipping."

"I thought you loved us."

"I do. Which is why I want you and Holly to come with me. We can figure out our next chapter together." I keep repeating this over and over in hopes that eventually she'll believe me. I take another step toward her, not liking that she refuses to turn and face me. "Violet. Please, come away from the cliff. I'm worried you'll fall."

"I've seen what men do," Violet says, her eyes on the canyon below. "They're cruel. They're ruthless. They truly are the devil in human form."

"Not all men."

She nods. "Yes, all men."

"Violet…" I take another cautious step toward her, but I don't want to get too close and startle her or have her try to take a defensive step away from me, causing her to fall. "Please come to me."

"You hated it out there," she says. "You hated it and didn't fit in. You told us about the stories around the fire, and now you change it? You can't take back what you said. You hated it! You told us so." She still doesn't step away from the cliff nor look at me. "You know Holly and I won't fit in either. But Holly's strong. She's so much stronger than me. She may be able to adapt. If anyone can, it's her." She pauses. "But not me. I'll never belong anywhere."

"You belong with me."

She shakes her head. "No, Ember. I don't."

"Do you want to stay here?"

"No. Scarecrow is a cruel man. And an evil man." She looks over her shoulder at me for the first time. Her eyes are dark and appear sunken in. "Don't you see? I have no home. I have nothing."

"You have Holly. You have me. You also have you."

I take one more step toward her, but this time she does move closer to the edge as a warning for me not to come any closer.

Fearing what she might do, my heart stops, and I struggle for the right words but decide I can only speak my truth. "You're right that I was miserable out there. You're right that I hated being away from Hallelujah Junction. We're different people— outcasts. We've lived different lives than the masses, and no matter who I met, no one truly got me. Even Christopher. He sees me the way he wants to see me but refuses to see the damage inside. He doesn't want to see the ugly, the pain, and the vileness that surrounds me. My past is suffocating and my future dim. He doesn't want to see that. But I need to move forward for me. For *me*. Just as you have to move forward for you. You."

"Move forward where?" Her voice is shrill, and I realize this is the first time I've truly heard her raise her voice. There isn't a shred of timidness laced within the words she speaks.

"I don't know. But I do know we can't stay here. We have to escape Papa Rich and Scarecrow, and we have to stop being held captive. It's time we're free."

She faces the canyon again and nods, taking a step toward the edge. "Yes, I want to be free."

"Violet!" I stop myself from lunging toward her, fearing that my action could push her over the edge. "Don't do it. I know you think all will be better, but don't. Please. Think of Holly. Think of anything but what's at the bottom of that cliff."

"Go inside, Ember," she says.

"I'm not leaving you. I'll never leave you. Trust me on that. Never."

She lifts her head and looks up at the sky, taking a deep breath. She extends her arms and says, "I've never been free. I've never truly been happy. It's time I stop the suffering. It's time. I have to escape the darkness, Ember. I hope you understand. I have to escape."

"Violet, I love you!" I shout, hoping I'm loud enough that Holly and Christopher will hear and come running. I need reinforcements. I need help. But I'm too scared to scream for help, because I feel it's all it will take for Violet to jump before Holly can see her do it. "Don't do this. This isn't your way out. It's not your way out!"

She looks over her shoulder and gives me a warm smile. "But it is."

Without hesitation, she flings herself over the cliff, disappearing into the mountain fog.

17

CHRISTOPHER

Never in my life have I heard such a blood-curdling scream before.

"Violet! No! Oh God, No!"

It's Ember's scream. Ember is screaming!

I bolt out the front door with Holly close behind. I know I'm running, but I can't feel my feet, and I'm not sure how I actually reach Ember at the cliff's edge. It's as if I somehow teleported at a hyper-speed. My heart beat once inside the house and then not again until I reached Ember and knew she was all right.

If you call the out-of-control, screaming woman I love all right.

"She jumped! Violet jumped off the cliff!"

Ember's lying on her stomach in the snow, her arms outstretched over the edge as if she can somehow pull Violet back to land.

I start to reach for Ember and take her into my arms, but then I see Holly charging toward us, her own horrific scream howling through the frigid air. I intercept her run, feeling as if she would also fling herself over the edge, following her sister to her death, if I don't hold her tightly.

"I tried to stop her! I tried to stop her!" Ember is clawing at the icy earth, madness taking hold.

"No! No! Violet!" Holly is beating against me with her tiny fists as she tries to free herself. "No!"

The sound of pain shattering through the sky stabs at every nerve in my body.

I'm rooted in place. I want to fall to my knees and help the woman I love, but Holly needs me more right now. And Violet... oh, God, Violet... there is nothing I can do to help her, but I can't help but feel if I lie on the ground and claw at the earth like Ember that I too can miraculously bring her back.

But there's no bringing her back.

She's gone.

Violet's gone.

I'll fight with Holly for hours if it means she won't follow her sister, but suddenly her pummeling of fists stop, and she wiggles out of my arms and charges away from the cliff, back toward the house. I see an extremely large man dressed in flannel and furs sprinting out of the thick woods, and Holly is headed straight toward him.

"Violet!" she screams. "She jumped. Oh my God, she jumped!" Her words turn to howls as she crumbles to her knees right in front of the stranger who swoops her up and cradles her in his arms.

He continues toward me, and I'm not sure if I should welcome this stranger or feel guarded. He's larger than me, thicker. He has a full beard, long hair, and is rugged, but he's not exactly dirty. It's clear from his appearance that he is not just a hiker or a camper. This is a man who has been living off the land. He has a deer hide around his shoulders, providing him warmth against the storm. Furs are underneath the leather, and flannel beneath that. He is layered and warm, prepared for the mountain as only a man who lives and breathes it can be.

"No... no... no..." Ember's cries bring my focus back to her. I bend down and pull her off the snow-covered ground and into my arms.

I don't say anything, because what can I say? But instead, I hold her shaking body close to my chest and place kisses on the side of her head. I want so desperately to take away her pain, but I'm completely at a loss as to how I can.

The mountain man reaches us and places Holly on her feet next to me. Holly stands in place and watches the man walk toward the edge and peer over the side. I'm nervous for him, since the snow and ice all around doesn't make the ledge a safe place for anyone to be. He falls to his knees and leans over more—so much so that I prepare myself to pull him back from his own death if I have to.

Holly—who hasn't moved—cries out, "Violet, why? Why?"

Ember clings to my shirt and sobs even louder.

"I think I see her," the man calls out. "She's down there. I see her."

I release Ember and charge toward the edge myself. "Alive?" I ask.

"I don't know… but she didn't fall all the way. A tree branch stopped her. She's caught in the tree."

Ember and Holly both start toward the edge, but I turn around and put out my hand to stop them. "Don't come any closer. It's slick here!"

"Is she alive? Oh my God! Is she alive?" Ember asks, her hand over her mouth, her eyes wide as she trembles in place.

It kills me to see the woman I love appear so unhinged. I want Violet to be alive for her own sake, but also for Ember's. I'm not sure she'd survive this if Violet truly is dead.

"Please tell me you can see if she's breathing," Holly calls out.

I lean myself over the edge, and the mountain man holds onto the back of my shirt to make sure I don't slip off. He's right. Violet is about twenty feet down or so, stopped by the large limbs of a cedar that has grown from the mountain.

"I see her!" I say as I try to focus on if she's moving at all or if I can see her chest rising. "I can't tell if she's breathing."

But then I hear a moan and see a slight movement of Violet's head.

"She's moving! She's moving!" I shout, turning my head to look at the man. I then refocus my attention on Violet. "Violet! Don't move. If you can hear me, you stay still! Don't move an inch. We're coming for you."

"She's alive?" Holly screams, running to the edge of the cliff, regardless of my warning. Luckily, Ember has regained some sense and is pulling Holly back to a safer distance.

"We'll get to her," I say, not sure exactly how we will, but no fucking way will I allow her to die down there alone.

She may have every single bone in her body broken, and death may be inevitable, but she'll die in her sister's arms, knowing she's loved. Not alone. Not cold. Not on the side of a cliff.

The stranger, who has yet to give me any indication as to who he is, says, "Go get us some rope. Quick!" His voice is gruff, as if he hasn't used it in years.

Holly spins on her heels and charges toward the house. I look up at Ember and tell her, "Don't worry. We'll get her."

Tears are flowing down her face, but for the first time since running out here, I see some sanity returning to her expression. Hope is soothing the madness away.

I turn to the cliff and scoot my belly a little closer so I can get a better look. I'm not sure how we're going to reach her, and I hope Mountain Man has an idea. I already know my phone isn't working, and the hike out of here will take too long. So, any chance of rescue will rest solely on us. Holly returns quickly with an armful of thick rope. It's dirty, tattered, and frayed in some places, but it does appear intact.

The stranger takes the rope from her and runs toward the nearest tree, which sadly is only an aspen, and not even a fully matured one at that. The thick-trunked pine trees are too far, and no way will the rope reach them. I'm not sure the aspen is strong enough to hold Violet's weight, let alone the stranger's or mine, but we don't really have a choice.

The mountain man must be thinking the same as me, because he calls out, "I'm not sure this tree will hold my weight. I'm going to need you to also hold the other end and try to bear the majority of my weight." He continues to tie the rope around the tree and looks up at me for confirmation that I'm on the same page as him.

Jesus Christ, we're doing this.

This man is going to throw himself off a cliff to rescue a woman who is barely alive, and I'm going to hold him with nothing but my weight and hopefully a well-rooted aspen tree.

Ember and Holly both run over to where I've just gripped the rope and take hold as well. We can use all the help we can get, because he is not a tiny man.

With the skill of a true outdoorsman, the man wraps the rope around his torso and begins to rappel off the edge without the slightest hesitation. The tug on the rope burns my hand, but I hold firm as I glance at the tree, which is also remaining steadfast.

"If this tree breaks, let go of the rope," I order the women. But I already know they won't, just as I won't. If Mountain Man goes down, we all do.

"I'm almost there," the man shouts from the other side. I appreciate his feedback, because not knowing makes this harder.

I scan the length of the rope and am happy to see that so far it's holding his weight as well.

"I've reached her," he yells up. "She's alive and conscious. I don't think she can make it up the cliff alone. She's pretty hurt. So, I'm going to have to tie her off with me. It might be too much for the rope—"

"We got you, man," I shout out, sweat beading on my forehead. I want to take as much of the weight as we can so we don't tax the tree until we absolutely have to. I'm terrified to hear the snapping sound of the bark.

"Please be okay. Please be okay," I hear Holly chant under her breath as she digs her heels into the snow and holds the rope with a strength that only a sister trying to save her sibling can do.

"Go ahead and start pulling," he orders from down below.

I can tell the minute Violet is added to the rope and the mountain man is climbing back up. I begin to pull with all my might, tearing at the flesh of my hands. Ember is yanking, Holly is as well, and slowly we are pulling them to safety.

Fresh snow begins to fall from the sky, but luckily it seems to not be sticking. The only sound is our heavy breathing and groans of exertion.

"Almost there," the man calls out. "I can almost reach the landing."

I pull harder with his words, knowing he'll need that extra heave to get Violet to the top.

"Ember, you let go of the rope on the count of three, go to the edge, and help pull Violet up when you see her. One. Two. Three!"

I dig my feet farther into the wet snow as I feel the rope give when Ember follows my command. For such a small woman, it's clear how much of the weight she was holding, because I feel my feet slipping a bit, and Holly and I both have to readjust our stance to pull even harder.

"I see them," Ember calls out. "Violet's eyes are open! She's alive. Alive!"

"Be careful!" I shout between clenched teeth. "Get down on your belly to reach out. Don't let their weight pull you over."

Grateful that Ember doesn't question my command, I watch her do exactly as I say. And within seconds, Violet and Mountain Man are cresting the impossible. His thick fingers grab the edge, and he climbs the rest of the way up, pulling Violet alongside him with Ember's assistance.

Holly and I both release the rope and run toward them.

"Violet! Oh God! Violet!" Holly is nearly hysterical.

Ember sits back on her butt, winded from the exertion. She's watching the sisters hug as tears run down her face.

Violet is weak, cringing in pain with every movement, but still able to give her sister the affection that none of us believed would happen again.

Feeling as if I can breathe for the first time since running out of the house, I walk to the stranger and extend my hand, helping him off the snow-covered ground.

"I don't know what to say, man. Thank you." If he hadn't come out of the woods... Violet wouldn't be alive. No way in hell could I have done that myself.

He nods, looks at Holly and then Violet, and starts to walk away.

"Wait!" Holly calls, jumping up and reaching for him. "You can't leave. Please stay. Please. Violet needs you now."

I get the feeling she knows the man—the way she ran up to him and now begs for him to stay. But at the same time, she knows it's unlikely he'd stay without her begging him to.

Ember is looking at Violet's leg. "I think it's broken," she says.

The man's face appears pained, and he kneels where Violet is lying and takes over examining her leg. When he moves it, she cries out in pain.

"We need to get her inside," I say, knowing she's been outside in the elements for too long, and aside from broken bones, we'll have to deal with hypothermia.

The mountain man reaches beneath Violet, swoops her into his arms, and begins trudging through the snow as if her body doesn't weigh a thing.

I reach down and assist Ember up. Her body is frozen, and I worry about her as well. I wrap my arm around her and say, "We need to get you warmed up too."

"Thank you," Ember says as we head back to the house. "You saved her life. You saved her, and you saved me. I couldn't have lived with myself if—" Her voice cracks, and a sob escapes her chattering lips.

I pull her closer to me and speed up our pace as the snow falls around us a little harder now. "She's safe now. All will be fine."

"Because of you," she chatters. "Everything will be fine only because of you."

18

CHRISTOPHER

"I didn't catch your name," I say to the man as we all stand around the fire, trying to warm our soaking-wet bodies.

The man looks at me but doesn't say anything. His long beard is wet, his clothing as well, but he seems steadfast and strong. I don't see a shiver in his body. His only concern and focus is Violet, who he's placed on blankets laid out by the fire by Holly in a mad dash when we entered the chapel.

"Do you live around here?" I press. I feel the need to get to know this man. Not because I don't trust him, but because there's a deep curiosity to find out who he truly is.

Ember is studying the man intensely as well. "You've been watching us, haven't you?" she asks. "It was you who I called out to, wasn't it?"

Ember's right; it's been him in the woods all along. "I saw you too, right? It was you who I saw and was yelling at."

He doesn't say anything but nods. It was never Richard or Scarecrow. It was this man... watching.

"You watch us and have been. That's how you knew Violet went over the cliff?" Ember adds. "You were watching the whole time."

"The mountain is no place for women to be left alone," he says as he runs his fingers over Violet's other leg and arms. "I think the only broken bone is your leg," he tells her. "I'll splint it if you'll let me."

Violet nods as she reaches out for his hand. "Thank you. Thank you for saving me... again." She then looks up at Holly and begins to sob. "I'm so sorry. I'm sorry I did that."

Holly kneels beside her and takes her hand in hers. "Shhh... you don't need to worry about that now."

Violet looks at Ember. "I'm sorry, Ember. I know I can never take back what I did. Why I did it... I'm sorry."

Ember takes her other free hand. "Promise me you'll never do this again. We love you, Violet. Nothing is ever so awful that you have to.... Promise me."

Violet nods but continues to cry.

I stoke the fire as Mountain Man begins to work on splinting Violet's leg, noticing the storm isn't letting up as I had hoped. I really thought I'd be hiking down the mountain soon, but now with Violet's condition, this plan is definitely going to have to be modified.

Ember returns her attention to the mountain man, then looks at Holly and Violet and clearly sees what I do. This man isn't exactly a stranger to the sisters. "Do you know this man?" she asks Holly.

Holly glances at him and nods. "We do."

"He saved me from a mountain lion," Violet says. "And he's been watching over us ever since."

"Why didn't you tell me it was him out there watching us?"

"He likes his privacy," Holly says, shifting her weight and avoiding eye contact with Ember.

"Scarecrow would kill us if he knew we've spoken to another man," Violet says. "So, we kept him secret." Her eyes look up at him lovingly. "But he's always looking out for us. If it weren't for him, we would have starved when Scarecrow and Richard left to find you. They didn't leave us with any food or means to hunt for any." She hisses in pain as the mountain man secures the splint tighter.

Ember smiles and shakes her head. "Was it you giving the rabbit and mushrooms to Violet a couple of days ago?" She shakes her head. "I was wondering how Violet could be so lucky to find all that."

"Do you have a name?" I ask again, liking the man but uncomfortable not knowing his name.

"Isaac." He sits Violet up and asks, "Do you mind if I run my hands up your spine and on your ribs? I want to make sure you didn't do any harm to them."

She looks toward Holly to make sure she's doing the right thing by allowing him to touch her even more than he already has.

"Go ahead," Holly says for her.

Violet cringes in pain when he touches her, but Isaac seems happy as he nods. "Nothing looks broken. Just bruised, which will still hurt like a son of a bitch."

Ember stands from her crouched position and walks over to me. She doesn't say a word but rests her forehead against my chest. I wrap my arms around her and pull her closer to the fire.

"I've never been so scared in my life," she says quietly to me. "I don't know what Holly and I would have done without you and Isaac." She tilts her head up at me. "But we can't leave. I know you want to. But with Violet hurt... and the reason she jumped was... it's my fault for her fall."

"No," Violet calls out, hissing when she moves too quickly, overhearing what Ember is saying. "Don't you blame yourself. Please don't. I don't know what got into me. It's just that sometimes I'm so sad. So... it feels like blackness covers me. Like a thick tar. I can't see hope. I can't see good. But this is not your fault, Ember. It's not. Please, please don't think that. I was stupid. Reckless. And God gave me a second chance that I will not take lightly."

"Why did you do it?" Holly asks, new tears falling from her eyes. "Why?"

"The thought of leaving was too much for me. I didn't want to go. But I didn't want to stay."

I notice Isaac look up at her and scowl, but he doesn't say a word.

"I feel lost in the woods with no trail," she adds.

"Well, right now, you don't have to worry about anything but healing. You'll have to stay off this leg for a while. No chores. No firewood gathering, and absolutely no hiking down the mountain," Isaac interrupts, still frowning.

Ember looks at me, and I nod in understanding.

We may be here a while.

But at the same time... we have to leave before Scarecrow and Richard return. We have a time limit, and my gut tells me we're running out of that time. Those men won't stay gone for long.

Isaac stands up, warms his hands by the fire, and says, "I'll be heading home. But if you need anything—"

"Please don't go," Violet says as Holly wraps a quilt around her shoulders. "It's snowing outside and getting dark. I can't live with myself if someone gets hurt because of my actions. Please stay with us. We don't have much, but we can make up a bed. Please."

"Yes, stay," Holly adds. "I don't know where your home is, but since we've never seen it gathering wood or foraging for food, I know it has to be far enough away that walking in the snow and at night isn't safe. So please. I'll start supper too. Stay."

Isaac looks at me, and I simply shrug. "Women have spoken. As you can see, I'm not going anywhere either. I think we're stuck here for at least the night."

For the first time, I see Isaac smirk as he nods. "You may need my help lifting Violet," he says, not saying yes but not saying no.

"Then it's decided," Holly announces, turning her attention to making supper.

Violet reaches out for Isaac's hand again. "Thank you, Isaac. I'm so happy to have you in my life. If it weren't for you—twice—I wouldn't have one."

He squats next to her and with his free hand swipes her hair away from her face. "Never again, little one. Do you understand? Never again."

She nods and swallows hard. "I'm sorry. I don't know why...." She begins to cry, and Isaac pulls her into his chest. "I don't want to leave. I don't want to stay. I don't want this life anymore. I don't know what to do."

"Shh," he says. "Everything's going to be okay. Just rest right now. Rest."

I watch Ember walk over to Holly and take her into her arms. Holly breaks down and begins crying into Ember's shoulder. And for the first time since arriving, I really see why Ember has been so torn about leaving. She truly loves these women. They truly are her family. And after what happened, after doing everything within my power to save her family and the tiny and broken woman lying on the floor... I can actually picture them as my family too.

Ember walks over to me eventually when Holly returned her attention to the supper preparation. I don't know if it's because everything was so bad, so awful, and so dark, but when Ember reaches for my hand and holds it tightly, I get an odd sense of warmth and comfort. Almost a sense of home. A glimmer of light shines through the black. At least for now. Right this second.

I have Ember, my wife.

I have shelter and a fire to keep me warm.

I have people around me who are only good and genuine.

I have simplicity.

For now... I can breathe again.

19

"Looks like the storm fizzled out last night," Isaac says from behind me.

It's first thing in the morning, after a long, sleepless night, and I'm questioning if today is the day for the descent or if tomorrow is a better day. I also can't figure out how we go about moving Violet, and I'm wondering if I need to go down by myself, get help, and take it from there. I don't want to leave Ember, but at the same time, I know she won't leave without Holly and Violet.

"I don't think it will last, however," I say, looking up at the sky and trying to judge if the clouds in the distance are storm clouds or not.

"Those clouds will bring snow," Isaac says, answering my question.

I sigh loudly, not sure what our next step should be. "It's refreshing here," I say. "Too bad this place is laced with evil."

"They don't want to go," Isaac says. "I think Violet's desperate act yesterday proved that."

"I understand," I reply, turning to face him. "I really do. But you don't know Scarecrow and Richard like I do. I can't in good faith leave those women here. And I also can't allow Scarecrow and Richard to leave for Wyoming and be free men. They're sick and belong behind bars. Which then leaves those women alone."

"I moved to these mountains about ten years ago," Isaac says as he looks out into the forest. "I live down the mountain some and near a river with a waterfall and large slabs of granite. It's my paradise, even though you may disagree. Violet and Holly see the beauty in this land like I do."

"It is beautiful," I agree. "But as you said last night —no place for two women to survive alone."

"True."

"You couldn't even leave them here alone," I point out. "You were helping and watching over them."

"True."

"So, you understand why I feel responsible for them."

"I do."

"And I have my wife to think of," I add. "Ember loves those women and will not leave without them."

"She wants to know they're safe," Isaac says.

"Of course. I do too."

"Do you have a plan? Where will you take them once you fly away from here?" Isaac asks, though I don't get the feeling he is drilling, judging me, or even accusing me of doing something reckless. I get the feeling he generally cares and wants to help.

"I don't know. I wish I had a concrete plan in my head, but I don't. I impulsively hopped on a private plane to get my wife back. I didn't have any idea what would happen after. And then when Holly and Violet were thrown into the mix." I release a deep breath. "I don't know."

"I think the women are picking up on that. I think they know you don't know what happens next. They sense it."

"But again, whatever we do is better than what's happening to them now. Those poor women… and no way in hell will I let Ember be here for another second without me."

Isaac takes a deep breath, inhaling the crisp mountain air. "When I sold everything I had to move up here, people thought I had lost my mind. I was crazy for wanting to leave a lucrative business, a lavish lifestyle, and basically the American dream realized. But you know what? I was miserable. Absolutely miserable. From the little I spoke with Ember last night, it sounds like her experience in New York was the same. I can relate to that. I hate New York with a passion."

I nod. "I won't be going back. Everything there and the people are dead to me. I'm here cleaning up a mess caused by *New York*, and I won't be repeating that mistake again."

"I understand that feeling. I left everything behind," Isaac says. "My past is dead to me as well."

"Christopher?" I hear Ember's voice call from behind me.

I turn to face her. "I'm out here talking with Isaac."

"Can you come inside? Holly and Violet want to speak with us."

I nod and all three of us go inside, where Holly is sitting next to Violet, who is propped up and already has renewed color in her face. She appears more comfortable and at ease, and it's obvious that a good night's sleep served her well. Holly also seems better. Last night, she fretted for hours, unable to settle and jumping every time Violet moved.

"We know you want to leave today," Holly begins as we all circle around the fire where they are. "And we know why you do and can understand that. But Violet and I spoke for hours last night while you were all asleep, and we came to a decision."

"We aren't going with you," Violet blurts.

Ember gasps, and I see tears well in her eyes instantly.

"But before you get upset or try to talk us out of it, I want you to hear us out," Holly cuts in, walking over to Ember and placing a hand on her arm. "Listen. Please."

"Our mother and father made a decision when we were children to live off the grid. They homeschooled us and taught us to live off the land. Our pa wasn't always a bad man, but when our mother died, he died too... or at least his spirit did. It got ugly then. Our life got really ugly. But the one thing Violet and I had was the beauty around us. We could see what our mother saw. We could love what she did. We could live the life she always dreamed of. She wanted us to live like this, and for the most part, we loved it too."

"But Scarecrow," Ember interrupts.

"Yes, he's awful," Violet says. "Which is why we aren't going to stand in your way of reporting him and Richard to the authorities. We actually hope you do so we never have to see him again. We want him to rot in jail for everything."

"So, what we are going to do is leave and find a hunting shack we know exists nearby. We will hole up there until after Richard and Scarecrow return and are hopefully arrested. In which time, Violet and I will return to the chapel—our home—and live off the land. We know how. We *want* to know how."

"Then I stay too," Ember blurts, which rips at my soul.

Holly shakes her head. "No, Ember. You belong with Christopher."

"We see that," Violet says with a warm smile. "We see how much you both love each other."

"But I love you both too," Ember argues, tears falling freely now.

"Then you come and visit," Holly offers. "Once everything settles and it's safe for you to do so. And who knows, maybe someday, Violet and I will want to leave this mountain, and it will be nice to know we have a place to visit as well."

"What if I find us a place in the mountains?" I suggest. "I could buy us some land, build a house—"

"We want to stay here," Violet says, her eyes stealing a glance at Isaac, who stands by and watches. "We have a good friend nearby, and we don't want to leave him."

"You're injured," Ember points out, swiping at the tears on her face. I can see her sadness is morphing into anger. "You both just experienced an awful ordeal and aren't thinking straight. It's winter! You don't have enough supplies, you can barely keep up with the firewood, and this chapel doesn't even have a completed or functioning chimney! I need you both to stop and think with your minds... not your hearts. I get it. You're scared."

"We're not leaving this mountain," Holly presses. "I'm sorry."

Ember whips her head toward me and then to Isaac. "Say something! Convince them that this is just another suicide attempt. You will die in some hunting shack while you wait out the winter!"

Isaac nods. "Ember's right. You can't leave here and go live in a shack. I know this mountain, and the closest hunting shack is still two miles away from here, and there's no way Violet can make it in her condition. Not to mention, there are no resources to live off of during this time of year."

"See!" Ember squeaks as she returns her attention to Holly and Violet. "Even Isaac believes you should leave with us."

"No," Isaac says calmly. "I didn't say that. I understand why they don't want to leave. I get why they want to keep this chapel and this land, but I don't agree with hiding out in the hunter's shack." He walks to Violet and squats down next to her so he can look her directly in the eyes. "I'd like to suggest that you and your sister come stay with me. At least until Richard and Scarecrow are no longer a threat. I have room, and I have the supplies to last us through the winter. I can also care for your leg during your mend."

Tears form in Violet's eyes, and she shakes her head. "I can't ask that of you. You've already done so much for us."

"I wouldn't be offering if I didn't want to."

"We know you like your privacy," Holly says. "We can't impose."

"You can, and you will," he says more firmly. He then turns to look at Ember and me. "I can take good care of them until we get the news that all is safe and those men are gone."

I nod and look at Violet, who is staring at Isaac as she silently cries. I then look at Holly and ask, "Is this something you would want? I'd feel better leaving you with Isaac. In fact, I think it's the only way I'll agree to not taking you both with us."

I walk over to Ember and take her hand in mine. I squeeze gently, knowing she needs my connection to help her get through this. I know she doesn't want to lose her friends, but at the same time, she has to understand what they're going through and why they're considering other options.

"Violet?" Holly asks. "What do you think?"

Violet keeps her eyes on Isaac. "It's too much. You're being too nice."

Isaac pats her good leg and smiles. "The way I see it, it will save me from having to hike in the snow every day to come up here and check on you ladies. You'd be doing me a favor."

Violet smiles warmly and then looks up at Holly. "What do you want to do?"

Holly glances at me and then at Ember. "Would you agree to leaving us with Isaac?"

I nod, then wait for Ember to finally answer, "I don't want to leave you. I'll miss you every day, but I also understand." She looks at Isaac. "Thank you for being here. Thank you for being there for them."

Holly then places her hand on Isaac's shoulder. "Thank you for your generosity. My sister and I would love to stay with you until the chapel is safe."

Isaac pats Violet's leg one more time and stands. "All right then. I have plenty of blankets, food, and supplies, but you ladies better pack your clothing and any other items you want. It's going to be awhile until you can return." He then turns his attention to me. "Do you mind helping me get Violet to my place before you and Ember make your journey down the hill?"

"It's the least I can do," I reply, more than happy to be of some use.

The man has become all of our savior. He gave a solution to a problem I didn't feel could be solved.

"Let's get a move on. We have a lot to do before it gets dark. My place will take about half a day with Violet."

As everyone scrambles to get to work, I take a minute to pull Ember into my arms and ask, "Are you all right with this?"

"It's what they want," she says, her voice cracking. "I want them to be happy. They deserve that."

"And I want you to be happy. What will it take to make that happen?"

She pulls away and looks into my eyes. "You," she states simply. "I just need you to make me happy."

20

EMBER

It had been a long day and a grueling hike getting the sisters to Isaac's cabin. Christopher and Isaac were able to carry Violet the entire way, while Holly and I carried the supplies. Once we had them settled into the cabin, Christopher and I decided it would be best to come back to the chapel before dark, spend the night one last time, and then head out for the meadow at first light. Though Isaac offered his place for us to stay, both Christopher and I felt we needed some privacy so we could figure out our own future. We still have so much to discuss, and we really need some time to just be us... one last time before the craze of starting our new life begins.

Goodbyes were hard, but we all promised to stay in touch. Isaac promised to watch over Holly and Violet until we get word to them that Scarecrow and Papa Rich have been arrested, and knowing this made it possible for me to walk away. As hard as it was to leave them, I know deep down that they are happy now. They are living their lives the way they want to and on their terms. I could never force them to do anything but.

"It's just me and you now," Christopher says as we enter the chapel.

"It's so quiet," I say, walking over to the fire that is only embers now. It won't take me long to get it raging again, and I get to work quickly before the room gets any colder.

Christopher comes up from behind and wraps his arms around me, kissing the side of my neck. "I know today was rough on you. But I'm proud of you. You put their needs before your own, and I'm proud."

"It was hard. I want them with us, but I also know how hard it is out there... in society."

"Which is why we need to come up with a plan so it isn't so hard for you. Starting with the fact that we aren't going back to New York. You won't ever have to see my mother again or have the media hounding you. Wherever we go, we're going to keep it secret. It will take a damn good private investigator to hunt us down, and if they do... we'll leave again."

His words fill me with so much hope for the future. "What about your job?"

"I'll get another job if I want. Money isn't an issue for me, as you know. I love taking photographs, and that doesn't have to stop just because I don't work for *The Rolling Stone*. I can take freelance down the road if we decide it works for us, or I can take pictures for pleasure. Regardless, as long as I'm with you, I'll be happy."

"And your mother? Can you really walk away from her?"

He counters my question with one of his own. "Can you really walk away from Papa Rich?"

"It'll be hard," I admit.

"And it will be hard for me. But it's something we have in common. We won't be the first couple to have to deal with toxic parents and figure out how to handle that. They both deserve to be in jail, and hopefully that happens."

"So where do we go?" I ask.

"Do you still want the desert?" he asks, clearly thinking of locations.

I shake my head. "No. I like what you said earlier about living in the mountains. Being up here in the trees... this place makes me happy. Could we maybe find a place nearby? I don't mean living off the grid, but maybe a small mountain town?"

He tightens his hold on me and kisses me on the neck again. "I love that idea. A cabin with a wood stove and a carved bear out front."

"Just ours."

"Yes," he agrees. "Just ours."

"Someplace that they can't reach us. Never again."

"Never again."

I spin around and press my lips to his, instantly feeling the fire ignite inside me. Funny how hope for a good future acts like an aphrodisiac.

"We're all alone," I whisper seductively. "Just you and me. We don't have to be quiet." I nibble his lip and lower my hand to his crotch, which is already hard to the touch. "We can be loud. We can be very, very loud."

"Careful," he playfully warns. "You're awakening the beast."

"Maybe I don't want to be careful," I say as I dip my fingers down his pants and lightly caress his pubic hair. "I happen to like the beast."

"Take off your clothes," he orders.

Without hesitation, something I know the alpha in him expects—immediate compliance—I stand back and, with as much grace as I can muster, remove each item as seductively as I can. I know we aren't in the sexiest environment, but I want to please him. I want him to feel the desire I have inside for him. I can't give him lingerie and high heels, but I can give him complete surrender.

Christopher sits back on the wooden table, crosses his arms against his chest, and gives a wolfish grin. I get the feeling he's enjoying what he sees.

"Stand naked before me," he commands once all my clothes are removed.

I do so without protest, loving the sense of seductive power I feel from doing such a simple act.

"Turn in a circle and allow me to see that ass of yours."

I do as he says, turning my back to him, feeling his eyes burn against my skin.

"Spread your legs wide." I comply. "Bend over so I can see you on full display."

I pause for a moment—forcing myself to block out the dark memories of what that command would bring in my past—but do as he asks, knowing my future is so much better.

"Spread your cheeks for me. I want to see the hole that I plan to claim."

My heart beats hard against my heaving chest, but I reach behind and pull apart the fleshy mounds of my ass. The cold breeze of the chapel caresses the most intimate of spots, sending shivers down my spine and over every inch of bare skin.

I remain in position and feel a drop of arousal run from my pussy to my thigh. I can smell my desire, and though I know his eyes are feasting on the sight before him, I can't help but feel a mixture of humiliation and desire in my stance. The push and pull of the two emotions seems to drive my need for more even higher.

I hear his footsteps approach. I remain in position, determined to stay that way until he gives the command to move.

I flinch slightly when I feel his palm on my ass. "Keep them spread," he growls.

I've come to recognize the sound of his voice that means my body will pay the price in the most wicked and delicious of ways. He morphs into a beast, and I know exactly the tone.

I hear it now.

"I want to fuck your ass. I want my cock buried in this tight little hole."

My heart beats so hard I can feel the pulse in my temples. I swallow back the lump in my throat, trying not to break the position I know he wants me to hold.

"I don't have lube," he says. "So, I'm going to fuck this ass with your juices alone."

Panic mixed with a forbidden desire to have him do just as he pleases rumbles within me.

He swipes his fingers along my pussy, collecting the wetness, and presses them past my puckered hole. He coats every inch of my hole, preparing it for entry with my desire only.

He moves me to the edge of the wooden table and presses me down to lie on my stomach against the cold surface. "I'll go slow, but this is going to have more friction and won't be easy."

I tense but nod. I want this. I want to feel him inside me in the most intimate spots of my body.

"I'll be gentle, but this will take some time for you to adjust. I can't slide in with as much ease. I need you to relax, submit, and open up."

"Is it going to hurt?" I ask.

"Yes. Just the way you like it."

I nod again. Yes, just the way I like it. Only Christopher truly understands my need for a darker touch. My hunger for a little edge.

He lowers himself over my back and begins to softly kiss the side of my neck, my shoulder, my earlobe—each kiss sending tingles to my throbbing pussy. His cock presses against the crease of my ass, and I know the soft caresses are only a ruse to trick my body into relaxing before the rough claiming of my ass begins.

"I'm scared," I finally admit.

"Breathe...."

"I'm scared it will hurt too much. It will be too dry," I admit, fearful of the unknown. "But no matter how much I cry out, don't stop," I direct. "I want it. I want to feel you fuck my ass with nothing preventing the friction. Make my ass raw," I murmur, knowing that my own primal beast inside has finally been unleashed.

He reaches down with his hand and guides his cock to my tight back entrance. Very slowly, and with so much control, he presses the tip of his dick past the tight ring. He pauses so I can get used to the initial shock, the spread, and the burn from only having my own slickness as lube.

"Relax. Open yourself to me," he groans in my ear, following the words with soft kisses to my neck.

He pushes farther, causing me to gasp. The bite, the stretch, the erotic feeling, it all becomes too much. I miss the lube. I miss the ease.

I shake my head. "You're too big for me. I think I'll tear without lube."

Christopher whispers in my ear, "Take a deep breath." I do as he asks. "Take another one, and relax your muscles. You need to trust that once I am fully inside you, it will feel good. Submit yourself, your apprehension, and your complete body to me."

He reaches a hand around my front and finds my clit. He expertly circles his finger around it, giving me the exact sensation I need to allow my ass to fully take him. I focus my attention on the pleasure his finger gives me and am able to ease the muscles of my anus completely, pushing back against him to drive him even deeper. Doing so allows his dick to fully be rooted in my ass balls-deep as I cry out his name in pain and in pleasure.

I've come to realize I love and crave the two feelings combined above all.

"That's it, Ember," he praises as he slowly pumps his thickness in and out. "Let me claim that ass of yours. Let me make you mine."

My bottom hole stretches to impossible levels and is dry without the lube, but I enjoy the stinging friction and look forward to every biting thrust he gives me.

His gentle thrusts become a little more aggressive. Each push drives slightly deeper than before. Tingles in my ass become sparks of ecstasy. My dark channel pulsates around his massive dick, and I scream out his name. Tears of surrender course down my face as I allow every sensation to swamp my body. I don't resist. I don't fight. I don't think. I simply am.

My mewls and whimpers bring on a few more driving thrusts, and Christopher finally ends the ass-fucking with a roar as he shoots his seed in my dry hole.

We remain frozen, bent over the table, our life still in flux, Papa Rich and Scarecrow still out there. But right now... this very second, we have calm. We have us. And I realize that is all I need.

21

EMBER

"They caught the sonofabitch!" Christopher announces, his eyes full of excitement and body tense with emotions as he hangs up the phone. "They have both Richard and Scarecrow in custody."

"Oh my God," I barely squeak out. "They found them?"

"They came back for you as we knew they would, and the Feds were waiting." He walks over to the television and turns on the news.

I stare in disbelief as I watch Papa Rich in handcuffs being escorted by police into a building. His head is up, shoulders proud, and not an ounce of remorse is present in his face. Commentary about capturing the Ghost Town Killer rings in my ear as I watch the man I believed I loved walk toward his end of destruction. No one can die from his hand any longer. No more misery can be cast down upon the poor, unexpected trespassers.

He'll never get to be a ranger again. Only a prisoner.

They cut away and show Scarecrow in a wheelchair being pushed through a media storm and surrounded by police. He looks pathetic with his one leg. They've removed the straw stuffing of his other leg, which I'm sure has him pissed off. They took his identity and his dignity by forcing him to be pushed in a wheelchair by someone else. I feel for the person escorting him. I wonder if he still smells like onions, body odor, and feces.

"Watching them both, so far away, almost seems like being cheated. I didn't get to see them arrested for myself," I confess.

"I know," Christopher says. "It took everything in me to not be up on that mountain waiting for their return. But at the same time, we have to move on.

We can't be held captive by them forever. They aren't part of our story anymore."

"This doesn't seem real," I say under my breath. "I thought they'd never catch him. Never."

Christopher walks up behind me and places his comforting hand on my shoulder as we watch together. "Agent Martinez told me that they're going to want us to testify. I'm going to get an attorney right away to handle everything for us and help guide us through this storm."

I look up at him, instantly in a panic. "But what about our home? Will the media find us? You said where we're at is secret. It's ours. Only ours."

I love being in our cabin with no reporters waiting outside. Is that all going to change?

"We're going to stay hidden the best we can. I'll have our lawyer be our point of contact, and though we may have to travel to testify, we'll deal with the media and authorities *away* from our house. Our home will be our sanctuary always." He leans down and kisses my forehead. "I promise. I like the peace and quiet here just as much as you do."

Christopher had kept his word the minute we flew off the mountain. We didn't go back to New York, we had no interaction with his mother, and he found us the cutest cabin in a small mountain town called Pinesville. The town consists of one market, a post office, a pet store, a barbershop, and some other small businesses. It's quaint, charming, and already feels like home. We've met a couple of the people who live in the town, but they all seem to keep to themselves as we do. It's friendly, but not overly so. And if they know who Christopher and I are due to the media, they aren't letting on that they do.

Christopher is taking nature pictures and seems to love it. We go on hikes, and he gets lost in snapping one photo after another. We've settled into a routine of love, happiness, and contentment that I never thought possible. But I always knew in the back of my mind it was temporary. We were working on borrowed time because Papa Rich would enter my life once again.

And here he is.

On the television, so far from me but also so close.

"I'm not sure I can face him," I confess, staring at the man who at one time was my only family. The only person in my life who meant anything. The man I believed to be my Papa Rich.

I don't recognize the man anymore.

And not because he changed. No... he's the same man. The same *evil* man.

I just have my eyes open now. I can truly see the truth.

He's not *my* Papa Rich anymore.

He's Richard. He's the Ghost Town Killer. He's a bad, bad man and was my kidnapper.

Christopher lets out a deep breath and begins rubbing my back. "I wish I could tell you that you don't ever have to see him again. But I know you and I will be key witnesses in his trial. He'll be in the courtroom when you have to take the stand."

"What about your mother? Will we have to see her?"

He continues to rub small circles on my back. "It's likely. She's now a part of this court case as well. There's no way she'll be able to walk away from this with her hands clean. No matter how much money and how many fancy lawyers she throws at this, she aided a wanted felon. It's a crime, and I don't see her not having to pay for what she did to you. But my mother is no longer my concern. She gets to deal with her legal issues on her own."

"Are we going to tell the authorities the truth about what she did?" I ask, prepared to lie if that is something Christopher wants.

Louisa is his mother, and I completely understand the pull of family and what they can make you do or not do.

"I've already told Agent Martinez everything. I'm not going to lie for that woman, and I don't expect you to either. She'll have to pay for what she did one way or another. Knowing her, it will just be through her pocketbook. She has a way of getting out of everything bad. But regardless, she lost me in the process. She's dead to me, just as Richard is to you."

I reach for the remote and turn off the television. I don't want to see his face or hear the grating voices of the reporters any longer. "It's been so nice the last couple of weeks here with you. I just don't want to see it end."

Christopher walks around me and sits next to me on the couch. He takes both my hands into his and looks me straight in the eyes. "It won't end. We may have to take a small detour, but we'll return to this. I love it just as much as you do."

"I'm afraid that once we go back to that life, you may realize you miss it all. City life could pull you back."

Christopher smiles. "I haven't missed a thing. I've been asking myself why I waited so long to do something like this. I've always loved the mountains and vacationed near here often. So, to be able to live here every single day... it's like a permanent vacation." He leans forward and kisses me. "I'm making this change for me just as much as I'm doing it for you."

"We need to let Isaac, Holly, and Violet know that the chapel is safe," I suddenly realize, wondering how long it will be for us to get out to see them all.

"I already made sure that happened," Christopher says. "The Feds want to keep us happy right now so we cooperate with everything they need from us. I asked them to send one of their men to Isaac's immediately. Once the dust settles, we'll head out there and visit. See how they are settled in and if they need anything from us."

I've missed the sisters like crazy and can't wait to see them again, but I also know it was impossible to go back before they captured Richard and Scarecrow. We had to remain in hiding for our safety as well as theirs. Plus, we didn't want to give any clues to Richard and Scarecrow that we had already fled the mountain.

"Christopher..." I begin, not sure I want to actually speak my thoughts out loud. "Do you think it's possible to see Pap— Richard before we are in the courtroom? I don't want to see him, but there's a part of me that feels I need the closure. I need to be able to say goodbye to him and that part of my life. I won't be able to do that if I'm on the stand and he's staring at me from across the room."

"I'll have our lawyer work on it first thing. I'm sure it can be arranged if it's something you really want."

"It's not something I want but something I feel I need to do."

"I understand," Christopher says as he stands. "I'll make the calls now and make sure we have the best lawyer in the country handling us."

22

EMBER

I used to be a scared girl. Actually... I used to be a terrified girl.

Everything made me worry. Every shadow haunted me.

I hid in a schoolhouse, not just because I was forced to, but because I didn't know how not to hide.

It was safe there, and I craved safe.

I still regret that I was too weak and too cowardly to help Christopher when he first arrived in Hallelujah Junction. I didn't have the strength it took, and no matter how badly I wanted to step in and do the right thing... I couldn't.

I will forever be haunted by all the poor souls Richard killed in the acid pits. I wish I could have saved them. I wish I could have prevented their deaths somehow. I wish I could have been a different person.

But somehow, with Christopher by my side, and with time, I've become the person I always thought it was impossible to be.

I'm not the scared little girl who was kidnapped at age five.

I'm not the terrified ghost hidden away in a dilapidated building.

I no longer look out from the inside, wishing for a life I'd never have.

I've risen from the ashes of the town I helped burn down.

I'm stronger for it. I'm better for it.

I am no longer the Ghost of Hallelujah Junction.

I'm Ember Davenport, and nothing and no one will crush my spirit again.

Yes, I considered not having this meeting over and over again. But I know it's something I have to face head-on if I'm ever going to be able to let go of Richard. No amount of therapy will be able to cure me of the darkness he brings and the suffocating grip he has over me. It's on me. I have to do this. I have to take the control back.

Christopher and I have been traveling hours to get to the jail that is holding Richard until trial, and though we're both exhausted from the drive and the rush of different emotions, I insist that we come straight here. I need this to stop lingering over me. I need it to come to an end now.

And as I sit down in a plastic chair facing a glass divider, waiting for Richard to be escorted into the room on the other side, I release the breath I've been holding. I know it's going to be hard, but I have no idea just how much until I see him in his orange jumpsuit take the seat in front of me. Even though I know there is no way he can reach me, and the only way he can speak to me is by picking up the phone, and that police are all around us, I still have a moment of wanting to flee. I still feel terror that this man can take me again and I'll have to live my life in captivity once again.

But I fight back against the urge to run, and I also refuse to let him see the flurry of emotions raging through me.

We both pick up our phones and bring them to our ears, our eyes locked together.

"Ember," he begins. "I was hoping you'd come."

"Why?" I ask.

Is it so he can try to control me from afar? Is it because he wants my help to secure better legal counsel? Is it because he wants to yell and blame this all on me? Or is it so he can make me feel guilty for being free when he isn't?

"I'm going to be in here for a really long time," he says calmly. "You're going to have to be a strong girl and live without your papa."

I slam my hand on the table and lean toward him. "No," I seethe. "Don't you dare treat me like a weak little girl. You are not my father. You've never been my father. Do you understand that? I'm not going to sit here and let you speak to me as if I'm nothing but a scared child. Those days are over. Over!"

Richard leans back, licks his lips, and gives me a smirk. "I see Christopher has gotten into your head. You've allowed the devil inside."

"You're the devil," I say, regaining my calm. "You always have been."

He shakes his head. "No, Ember. I saved you. I raised you. It's because of me that you're even here breathing."

I take another deep, calming breath. "It's because of you that I missed out on life. You held me captive in a schoolhouse, tricking me into believing that it was all there was. You made me believe I had no other choice. You kidnapped me. That's the reality. You kidnapped me and trapped me in your own version of hell, just like you did to Christopher."

"I should have never brought that man into your life," Richard spits. "I'm paying my penance for that mistake now."

"You're paying your penance for all the people you killed and for all the bad that you did."

"Hard decisions have to be made in life," he counters. "You'll see this soon enough."

I nod. "Yes, I know all about the hard decisions. Coming here to face you was a hard decision, but I had to come. I had to look you in the eye and say goodbye. You won't see me or hear from me again after today. Not until I take the stand and help put you away for life, or to aid in giving you the death penalty if that's what's decided. I'm not your daughter. I'm not that barefoot little girl in Hallelujah Junction anymore. I never will be again."

"Christopher Davenport has corrupted you. I know this. I know this isn't really you speaking. You'll come around."

He's trying to act like my words mean nothing and aren't bothering him, but I can see in his eyes that they are. He's losing. He sees this. He hears it. And soon, he'll have no choice but to face it.

I shake my head and give my own smile. "No, Richard. This is not him speaking. It's me. All me. And I want you to know that you did one good thing for me. One. You gave me Christopher. He's a good man. He's my husband in all ways and forever will be. I have you to thank for that, but only for that one act."

"Don't let the devil stay inside you, girl."

Irritation prickles my skin. He'll never hear me. Not really. He'll sit there behind the bars of his cell and never see me for the new woman I am. No matter how much I try, I'll only be wasting my breath. I see this now. And the truth of the matter is...

I don't need him to see me for the strong and resourceful woman I've become.

I don't need his approval or his blessing.

I don't even need his understanding that I will never be in his life again.

I don't need anything from this man.

"You're going to spend the rest of your life looking out a small window at a freedom you will never have. You are going to be held captive. You are going to be at the mercy of your jailer. You are going to die knowing exactly how I felt. You are the captive now. Not me. I'm free. I'm finally free."

I hang up the phone and stand up to leave. I see his lips moving in rebuttal, his face red that I have the audacity to end the conversation before he's finished, but I couldn't care less what he's trying to say. I'll have the last word.

Me.

I'm in control. Not him. Never again will I hand my strength over to another person.

I walk out of the jail to join Christopher, who has anxiously been waiting for me. He doesn't see me when I first arrive, and he's pacing back and forth. The minute he does see me approaching, he runs up to me and takes me into his arms.

"Are you okay? How was it?" He pulls away so he can study my face.

I release the last breath of tension that is locked inside me and smile reassuringly. "He's a sick man. He's an evil man. But I know now that I'm free from all that. I never have to have him in my life again. It's over. It's finally over."

Christopher pulls me into a hug and kisses the side of my head. "Yes. You're free now, Ember. And I swear to you that you'll never have to go through that again. I love you; I'll always love you, and nothing and no one will ever change that."

Yes, I'm finally free. The Ghost of Hallelujah Junction no longer haunts the town.

EPILOGUE

EMBER

"They're here!" I hear Violet scream from the doorway of the chapel. "Holly! Isaac! Ember and Christopher are here!"

We reach the top of the mountain, winded from our hike but thrilled to finally see our friends again. Winter has passed, as well as spring, and the signs of summer are all around us. New life, new birth, a new beginning. The hike up to the chapel was far harder than the hike down, but I had the excitement of seeing them driving me forward.

Holly and Isaac follow Violet as they meet us halfway. I've never seen the sisters look so happy.

They have put on some weight, don't appear hollow and sad in the slightest, and I see smiles on their faces until their cheeks run out. Violet is the first to reach us as she throws her arms around me and pulls me into a tight embrace. She shows no signs of her once having a broken leg and in fact looks to be in perfect health and fitness.

"I've missed you so much," she squeals.

I see Isaac extend his hand to Christopher, and they shake and then hug like long-lost buddies. A bond has been forever formed between them, and it's obvious to see.

Holly forces Violet out of the way and gives me a hug herself. "It feels like forever since we've seen you," she says. She pulls away and scans my body from head to toe, smiles, then looks at Christopher. "Come on inside, out of the sun. Let's get you something to drink and eat. I'm sure the trip up here wasn't easy."

"That sounds great," I say, looking at the chapel with new eyes.

It doesn't have the haunted, evil, ominous look it did when I first laid eyes upon it. It's obvious that repair work has been done to the exterior. There are no longer gaps between the weathered wood.

Dead weeds that used to kiss the edges of the foundation are now colorful wildflowers.

When we enter inside, I almost don't recognize it. Log walls have been built, sectioning off rooms, instead of the tattered sheets we used before. The floors are clean, the windows sparkling, freshly cut flowers are in a mason jar in the center of the large table, and the chimney is complete. It feels like a home rather than a prison. It smells of Holly's stew, but this time it's being cooked over a hearth that appears expertly built.

"You've done so much to the place," Christopher says, spinning around and taking it all in. "It doesn't look like what I remember at all."

"It's beautiful," I add. "It really feels like a home."

Violet nods, walks up to Isaac, and takes his hand in hers. "Isaac helped us fix it up. We even have a well now with the freshest mountain water!"

Holly walks over to a pitcher of this water and pours us some glasses. "We couldn't have done this without him."

Isaac pulls his hand out of Violet's but replaces it by arranging his arm over her shoulders in a possessive embrace. I notice how Violet's cheeks pinken as he does so, and her smile beams even brighter. "I'm not taking any of the credit. These ladies know how to work hard. Once Violet's leg healed, she was up and at 'em like a tornado. I couldn't keep her down."

My heart warms as I watch Violet press her body to Isaac's. Holly doesn't seem to notice or care, which tells me this act is part of their normal day. Something has happened—a connection and closeness between Isaac and Violet—and I can't wait to get Violet alone so I can hear all about it.

We all settle in around the table and have small talk at first, but then it's Holly who finally says what we have all been waiting to discuss. "I can't believe they found both of them guilty. It almost seemed too easy."

"This nightmare is over," Christopher inserts. He reaches under the table, puts his hand on my thigh, and squeezes. "It hasn't been easy and nearly broke us at times. But it's finally over."

"It almost doesn't seem real sometimes," Violet adds. "I still keep expecting Scarecrow to walk through that door at any moment, demanding his supper."

I watch Isaac place his hand over hers and pat reassuringly. The brief moment of sadness that washed over her face vanishes the minute he touches her. All I see is pure happiness and bliss. I've never seen Violet look so alive.

"We can move on with our lives now," I say, happy that the trial is finally over.

Though our bulldog of a lawyer managed to shield us from a lot of the media madness, it still was a lot to take. Our privacy, however, remained intact, and our home is still our secret. It's pretty obvious that the townsfolk know who we are now if they didn't already, but they don't bother us about it. And with time, I'm sure they will move on to another's gossip. But we've started to make friends and settle in. Roots are growing, and I actually use the term "home" and mean it when I say it.

"Violet," I say, standing from the table. "Why don't you and I go get some firewood." I look to the full stack by the fireplace and smile. "For memory's sake."

Violet hops out of her chair and readily follows me. When we shut the door behind us and head to the barn, I get straight to the point.

"What's going on between you and Isaac?"

Violet blushes and looks down at her feet. "I like him. I like him a lot."

"It appears he feels the same way."

Her eyes dart up at me. "Really? You think so?"

I nod and smile. "I do. It's pretty obvious there is something there between you two."

"He took such good care of me when my leg was broken. Holly and I couldn't have survived without him. He's such a good man."

I gather an armful of wood and head back to the chapel. "He truly is. I owe him everything."

Violet reaches for some of the wood in my arms to lessen the load. "I know I wouldn't be here with my second chance at life if it weren't for him."

I pause before the door and turn to her. "Then take hold of what makes you happy. You deserve it. If Isaac is who you want, then grab on and never let go."

"I will," Violet promises. "I know what a gift I have now that I get to live life... and be happy. I won't throw it away ever again."

We both enter the chapel as if nothing of importance was discussed and easily join the group conversation as if we hadn't even left.

"Are you all still happy living up here?" Christopher asks, although we both already know the answer to that question. We can see it in how they look and how much work has already been done to the chapel. "My offer is still on the table to move you wherever you want. Pinesville is a great mountain town that Ember and I love calling home. You could join us there."

Violet's eyes dart to Isaac and then to Holly. "We've never been happier."

"Yes," Holly says. "We appreciate your offer, but we're really turning this place into our home."

Isaac chimes in with a proud sparkle in his eyes. "I've managed to purchase the property the chapel sits on. It connects to my own land, and so it was easy to just expand."

"What about you two?" Violet asks. "What are your plans? You just mentioned living in Pinesville. Are you going to stay? Raise a family someday?"

"Well, that's one reason why we're here," I answer as I reach for Christopher's hand. "I know you don't want to move from here, but we were hoping you'd at least come visit us in Pinesville for our wedding. Christopher has officially asked for my hand in marriage, and we're going to make our wedding vows legal. It's the last step of erasing our past and what was forced upon us. We are choosing to be married now. I want our vows to be made without an actual chain around our ankles."

"It would mean a lot to have you three there," Christopher adds. "You're our family."

"We wouldn't miss it for the world," Violet announces. "Oh, what amazing news."

When both Holly and Violet squeal in joy and pull my hand out of Christopher's so they can see the large diamond ring he bought me, Christopher and I both laugh at their excitement.

"You both look really happy," Isaac says. "It didn't come easy, but well worth the wait, it seems."

"I wouldn't want to go through this journey with anyone else—hard or not," I admit, looking at Christopher with so much love in my heart that it actually physically feels tight.

Christopher puts his arm around me and pulls my chair closer to him as he says, "It's about time I *truly* make Ember my bride. She was my captive bride, then my kept bride, and then my taken bride. But it's about time for her to be my forever bride."

· · ·

The End.

What's next? I have some secrets of what book is coming soon...

Be sure to sign up for my newsletter so you can be the first to know.

Alta's Newsletter

ALSO BY ALTA HENSLEY

Secret Bride Series:

Captive Bride

Kept Bride

Taken Bride

———

Top Shelf Series:

Bastards & Whiskey

Villains & Vodka

Scoundrels & Scotch

Devils & Rye

Beasts & Bourbon

Sinners & Gin

———

Evil Lies Series:

The Truth About Cinder

The Truth About Alice

Breaking Belles Series:

Elegant Sins

Beautiful Lies

Opulent Obsession

Inherited Malice

Delicate Revenge

Lavish Corruption

Dark Fantasy Series:

Snow & the Seven Huntsmen

Red & the Wolves

Queen & the Kingsmen

Kings & Sinners Series:

Maddox

Stryder

Anson

Prima

Mr. D

Mafia Lullaby

Captive Vow

Naughty Girl

Bad Bad Girl

Delicate Scars

Bride to Keep

His Caged Kitty

Bared

Caged

Forbidden

For all of my books, check out my Amazon Page!

http://amzn.to/2CTmeen

ABOUT THE AUTHOR

Alta Hensley is a USA TODAY bestselling author of hot, dark and dirty romance. She is also an Amazon Top 100 bestselling author. Being a multi-published author in the romance genre, Alta is known for her dark, gritty alpha heroes, sometimes sweet love stories, hot eroticism, and engaging tales of the constant struggle between dominance and submission.

As a gift for being my reader, I would like to offer you a FREE book.

DELICATE SCARS

Get your copy now! ~

https://dl.bookfunnel.com/tnpuad5675

I was going to ruin her.

I knew it the moment I laid eyes on her. She was too naive, too innocent.

I would wrap her in the darkness of my world till she no longer craved the light... only me.

I should walk away, leave her clean and untouched... but I won't.

I hold her delicate heart in my scarred fist and I have no intention of letting go.

———

It all started with a book... doesn't that sound crazy?

For your entire world to come crashing down around you over research for a book?

But that is what it felt like the moment I met him.

My world tilted. Nothing made sense any more.

I only know he became like a drug to me... and I shook with need till my next fix.

———

Join Alta's Facebook Group for Readers for access to deleted scenes, to chat with me and other fans and also get access to exclusive giveaways:
Alta's Private Facebook Room

———

Check out Alta Hensley:
Website: www.altahensley.com
Facebook: facebook.com/AltaHensleyAuthor

Twitter: twitter.com/AltaHensley

Instagram: instagram.com/altahensley

BookBub: bookbub.com/authors/alta-hensley

Sign up for Alta's Newsletter: readerlinks.
com/l/727720/nl

THE SECRET BRIDE SERIES

CAPTIVE BRIDE:

You will take this bride.

To have and to hold from this day forward.

Till death do you part.

This will be your solemn vow.

You have no choice.

Trapped in a twisted and dark courtship with a secret woman who needs my strength to survive, I will be wed.

Walking the thin line between lunacy and reality, I am now the protector of my future captive bride.

So, I have no choice but to recite the vows.

I take thee.

In this arranged matrimony.

Until we are parted by death.

KEPT BRIDE:

My history is forbidden.

My story, dark and twisted.

My future decided.

I know I don't belong in this decadent world—his
world.

Money, power, and dark secrets surround me now.

I submit to it all to be his perfect obedient wife.

They stalk my every move, watching me, judging me.

I'm in the same prison just with different guards.

But all I care about is him.

His eyes, his touch, his hold over me.

I'm forever his kept bride, even though they all try to
steal me away.

TAKEN BRIDE:

Secrets must be kept.

Vows never broken.

Till death do us part...

Unless everything changes.

Captive in one life...

Kept in another...

Taken to now be the wife I am forced to be.

I'm hidden away to face a dark reality only a few can survive.

But I have a purpose now. I can be the good wife I strive to be.

But he still wants me.

He will hunt me down.

He will find me and take back what was stolen.

I will be his wife if he has to fight until the death to make it happen.